EVEN THAT WILDEST HOPE]

yward Goodhand

[EVEN THAT WILDEST HOPE]

Seyward Goodhand

Invisible Publishing
Halifax & Picton

Library and Archives Canada Cataloguing in Publication

Title: Even that wildest hope / Seyward Goodhand.
Names: Goodhand, Seyward, author.
Description: Short stories.

Identifiers: Canadiana (print) 20190156627 | Canadiana (ebook) 20190156740 | ISBN 9781988784366
   (softcover) | ISBN 9781988784403 (HTML)

Classification: LCC PS8613.O634 E84 2019 | DDC C813/.6—dc23

Edited by Bryan Ibeas
Cover and interior design by Megan Fildes | Typeset in Laurentian
With thanks to type designer Rod McDonald

Printed and bound in Canada

Invisible Publishing | Halifax & Picton
www.invisiblepublishing.com

We acknowledge the support of the Canada Council for the Arts and the Ontario Arts Council.

Thus violence obliterates anybody who feels its touch. It comes to seem just as external to its employer as to its victim. And from this springs the idea of a destiny before which executioner and victim stand equally innocent, before which conquered and conqueror are brothers in the same distress.

—Simone Weil, "The *Iliad*, or the Poem of Force"

ENKIDU

He experienced all troubles with me;
Enkidu, whom I love so much,
Experienced all troubles with me.
He suffered the fate of mankind.

        —Gilgamesh, Old Babylonian Version, Tablet X

HOW CAN A MAN WITH LOVE IN HIS HEART do the evil that I have done?

Where is my radiant friend, where is Gilgamesh? What will he think of me now that I am dead and can no longer keep pace with him?

He will grow old while I stay the same. He will ask himself, when years pass, and knowing, as I do, that old men sometimes outgrow the companions of their youth: Do I still love Enkidu? Enkidu, with whom I committed murder. He leaves a bitter taste in my mouth. Thinking of him, I am ashamed.

Wisdom never came to me. I was a man full of ardour, who loved to play. Great love filled my heart when I saw my playmates. I was not picky—I could be friends with anyone so long as their hearts said, Yes, yes, yes, yes!

Now I am alone in a region of salt. Eyeless, tongueless, I crawl along the floor of the dream of my life. Nobody sees me, nobody hears my story. I tell it to myself but can find no meaning. If I tell it again, will my friend hear me?

❧

Before Gilgamesh found me, before he ever dreamed of me, I remember the quenching of thirst. I remember when the yellow hills of the uplands fell away against a sky so empty I would scream and leap into it, and always land on my feet running. Wild man-beast of the uplands, I roamed the yellow foothills of the Zagreb Mountains while, in the Sumer Valley below, Euphrates bore black ships filled with precious metals to all the cities. To fierce Akkad, to Babylon the fallen, to Nippur, where the wind lived in a house. But none as great, in my time, as Uruk.

My place was a ring of crags circling a water hole. I was friends with trees, rocks, everything, most of all the moon. My sisters were a herd of gazelles and these were their names: Bounce-With-Birds, Honey-Licker, Starless, Fawn-Drop, See-Far, and my favourite sister, Splash. My mother was a demon who had given birth to every species in the world. That was what I understood of my life.

Yet my anxiety was there, even from the start. I'd bend over the water hole, see my black-bearded face with its backless eyes, and feel such shame that I had to throw myself into the joy of my herd. Who could have guessed I wanted glory?

❧

One day, while swimming around with my sisters, I looked up, and there he was, standing at the edge of the water.

What a marvel! His beard was magnificent. Four braids: one crusted with lapis lazuli, another with carnelian, the third with black-and-green-banded agate, and the last shimmered with the ground-up dust of the pappardilû-stone. His chest and arms and huge bald head shone so golden I thought the secret veins of a cave had come to life and formed a man.

"Who tore off the skin of the world?" I growled.

My sisters bolted higher into the hills, except for Splash, who leapt behind me.

He shook his bright head and laughed. He had such a calm and delighted curiosity.

Once my eyes adjusted to his luminousness, I realized it wasn't his gold or gems but the way he possessed himself that had startled me. Call it brilliance. Well, I had never seen brilliance, except for my mother's, and she was a wild demon with a face like intestines. Imagine brilliance, but paired with a beauty like his! He was so superior to me, and astonished me so with the way he looked at me and assessed, I had no space in me for envy or indignation. All I wanted was for him to tell me who I was. Right away I had the faith in him that men have in Gods.

Lifting a bright arm, he pointed at my door.

I had leaned it against a tree called Old Olive, who grew on my dullest crag, so I could see it from afar. Just a simple door of grey cracked wood, no pole or pivot. But to me it was a wonder, a thing that divides one place from another. I'd stolen it from his trappers.

He stepped his huge foot sideways into the shadow of that door, bent and pounded his fist on its shade. "Knock knock," he joked.

Splash bashed into my rear, and splat went my face in the mud. "Go, play at the water hole, run through the grasses," she snorted.

"Baha!" he laughed, slapping his chest. "Bahaha!"

Mortified, I got up. That Son-of-the-Sun. We each stood at our height, two giants.

Above us crows cawed. "Better watch, better watch."

A haunted look came into his eyes and his begemmed beard quivered. "Wild man," he said. "I have your name, I brought it with me. It is Enkidu."

"Enkidu?"

"So you're the one my trappers told me about. Like a God's testicle dropping from the sky, no one can budge you, eh? You run in the throng of beasts with delight in your heart. Who can blame you for filling in the pits of hunters and pulling up snares? How would you know what I need, you milk-sucking king of the hairy-priests? You are so handsome and strange. That black hair on your head is long as a woman's, yet fur covers your whole body. On the one hand, you move gracefully; on the other, you're thick as a tree. Your eyes are like clay, hot in the kiln. And look at that hooded cock. Is it big or is it small? But then those breasts. They're making me thirsty. Tell me, why did you steal the door to my trappers' lodge and mount it high on a cliff for all to see? That's how I found you, you know. I followed your footprints up the mountain to this door against the sky."

My cheek got hot and I scratched it. I loved that door, which was not unlike Old Olive, who endured forever, rooted in her spot, eyeless and unaware but intimate within herself. I was born lacking intimacy within myself, but now I had something of it in my door. It was my first trophy and I chose where it would go—unlike the crags and trees and streams and sky, which were responsible for themselves—and because of that, I felt a part of me always remained at home, waiting for the rest of me to return.

His casual-but-exposing manner! "Miracle man," I said. "You may be tall and bright, but my bones are bigger!"

I didn't know yet how sensitive he was to bravado.

He raised his bow and shot Splash through the neck. She fell at my feet and I fell with her, whimpering in the mud.

"Forgive me, Enkidu," he said gently. "Usually I respond to such affronts by pulling out a man's eye and showing him his own face. I have no choice in that. But I do not wish to hurt you more than I have just done. I am no poacher. I am Gilgamesh, King of Uruk. My mother is a God and I have divine intelligence. Mighty Enkidu, allow my trappers to do the work of the wild, and in exchange I invite you to come with me to dig a well down to the Land of the Dead. You're the one I've dreamed about. You will save me with your friendship and I will love you as if you were my wife. Come with me and I swear the wild will have a place for itself in the Land of the Dead."

"What's the Land of the Dead?"

He laughed. "Between you and me, it's Fame."

"And what's that?"

He watched me quietly before answering. "Fame is existing in other people's minds. The more minds you exist in, the more real you are. I'm the realest man on this earth. Or so I thought, until I found you. How is it that you have a density like mine? Why can I see you?"

On top of my crag, Old Olive listened, black against the sun, eating light with a self-sufficiency that frightened me.

All my life, I ran the yellow slopes dreaming that the countryless world I knew so well—the steep crags and grassy scarps, forests so tall with unsleeping time in the roots the seat of nature grew in them, gibbering with the music of beasts all the way to the gulf—that they loved me for protecting it. But when he said Enkidu, the world no longer seemed like a bright intuition I leapt around in.

7

All at once, I saw the wild as a precious rock to hold in my hands—who but me had a possession like that?

Anxious that he would find me spineless and forsake me, I slung Splash over my shoulders and ran around the water hole after him. Loin-girded, sure-strided shepherd of men, he glided down the hot hills singing a lamentation song, mournfully drumming the leather of his arrow bag. He knew I loved my sister more than a man normally loves a gazelle, and he wanted to be generous with his regret.

Soon we came to the trappers' stone lodge, which sat in its yard toppled like a tooth. A quiet sigh seemed to speak to me:

Now who trembles in his very core? He has a name now— Enkidu.

And then a bird screamed the words the trappers had cried as I hanged them by their feet:

God-man, my God, I swear I worship you, not that one down in Uruk, I swear I've always worshipped you.

The spindly contraptions where they'd hung meat over low fires to smoke lay in pieces, and the mounds of dead lions wrapped in palm fibres went so fast with maggots I couldn't believe it. The trappers still hung from boughs by their twisted shins.

At the entrance to the stone lodge, Gilgamesh fingered one of the broken leather hinges where I'd torn off my door. He spoke shyly, as if amused. "I'll admit, Enkidu, when the trappers who got away came begging me for help against the wrath of a God-man, I laughed. Another God-man? Now I see you carrying that gazelle down a mountain as easily as if she were a nut on your shoulder. I've never met anyone who is the same size as me. The carnage you wrought here is an abomination. Yet I admire your power, and I find in it something endearing. You see, I too have a temper."

He kicked a stone loose from the doorway. His eyes averted, he grabbed my beard with a golden hand. He led me silently by the beard down a well-trodden path through a juniper forest, until we came onto a steppe. Through a grove of strangler figs, swarms of men with shiny black braids straight out behind them raced chariots at each other, swerving at the last second.

"These are my soldiers," he muttered. "See how measly they are?" He threw back his head and opened his throat to them. "So, have you found the path, have you found the dim gate down to death?"

Hearing him, his soldiers raised their dirks and chanted, "Ho, ho!"

Then they saw me. They steered their horses over. All those piles of eyes looked up at me.

"He's as huge as Gilgamesh," they said.

He went to the rim of a freshly dug hole, and I followed, looked down. More eyes peered from the dark, and then a splash of muddy water shot up—his men below were throwing it.

"Enkidu," he said, scraping shit off his sandal with an arrowhead. "I'm looking for a gate to the Netherworld. But the whole place seems to be surrounded by an enormous river I've called Huber. Well, too bad for them. We'll pump it out. Good for irrigation anyway."

But me, I was crying. "My sister is stiff. I want you to undo it. I want Splash to be soft again."

He put his golden hand on my arm. "All right, Enkidu. I offer condolences for that gazelle and decree the Netherworld also has wilds upon which she will roam for the rest of eternity."

Arms outspread, he turned to face his men.

"And I decree that the Netherworld's wilds are not the site of a massacre, but a range of Holy Mounds with their own protective deities—pilasters sculpted from a dragon's rib cage—with Enkidu as governor and temple administrator. All gazelles dear to Enkidu's heart shall have their horns carved into good omens and live in sound judgment on those Wilds of No Return, a blessing on their heads."

He dropped his arms and curtseyed, pleased with his generosity but also mocking himself. Then he took my hand and pulled me through the figs, onto a ridge.

Now my eyes stretched wide. Here was a view I'd never seen.

Down below, under a veil of mist, Euphrates ran her muddy veins through a giant litter of barley fields, arable tracts, canals glutted with carp, irrigated orchards.

He waved his arms, as though conducting the ships that entered the quay one after another. "Look, that ship there is the Meluhhans, bringing me my elephants and the crushed mollusc that makes crimson. That one is sailing out to Nippur from primeval Eridu—one must drink only the wine of Eridu! And there, see how the Palace of Head in Heaven floats over my city on its terrace."

When I asked him if he'd made a mountain, he laughed.

"No, Enkidu, you wild baby. I took clay and invented something called a brick. And between all the layers of bricks sits an ancient *giparu*—the same wedding mat Gods conceived the morning star upon. Uruk is built on the fornication of planets."

Inside the red walls, the Houses of Heaven—glazed in blue lapis lazuli and white quartz—sat halfway to the sky on terraces of monumental limestone stairs. All around, specks hauled loads nearly as large as themselves to and from the bases of towers so smooth of shape they looked more like thoughts than things. Roofs rose before my eyes and roofs fell apart. I could not tell Uruk's creation from its destruction, though the brightness of both events pierced my heart.

Gilgamesh explained that the specks had enamelled his tiles with gold and zinc, to rival the Gods that wander the stars at night. If he could build a ziggurat that moved all year in an orbit around the city, that would be ideal.

Stone highways wide as the river ran out in all directions, and on those highways spun thousands of wagons hauling piles of sesame. A square-mile date grove, a square-mile claypit, a square-mile city, half a square mile of palace.

In a field outside the walls, soldiers trained under their generals, and the generals under their captains, and the captains under the seven overseers of Uruk, each overseer responsible for a car of 25,200 men. One hundred and eighty-thousand soldiers turned at the same time and flashed their shields, like a smack of jellyfish rising on a wave.

"Soon they will go to Akkad," he said. "They will make Akkad a haunted place."

"Why?"

He moved his long blue nails across all those tiny people. Holding his city in one hand, he squeezed his palm as if it held a beating heart.

"*Tha-thum, tha-thum*, eh, Enkidu? *Tha-thum.*"

He paused.

"This is the world of the living. And yet. Enkidu, can you see the Land of the Dead in Uruk's shadow?"

I shook my head.

He pointed up at invisible black mountains and down at invisible gulfs, and at the absent sphere of darkness over them, *the sun in its aspect of death*, he called it. But all I saw was Uruk, the real Uruk, which looked enough like a dream to me—why would he need a nightmare on top of a dream?

"Doesn't it ever haunt you, Enkidu?"

"What?"

"The beating heart of the not-yet."

I shrugged.

"What will the unborn do, Enkidu?"

"Do?"

"What will they *do*?"

Just then, the sun mounted the sky and struck the Palace of Head in Heaven, covered in gypsum plaster to make it burn the eyes of enemies across the plain—as many blinding blades as stars gored the Valley of Sumer. His men knelt along the ridge.

Eyes wide, Gilgamesh stared at the temple, took in all the rays, looked deep into his dream. And who was there, who was there deep in his dream—wasn't it me, Enkidu?

The sun crested its peak. The blades of light returned to their sheaths.

"Enkidu does not bow to brother Shamash? I thought I was the only man equal to the sun."

"I do not bow," I told him, though I did not know what bowing was.

He narrowed his green eyes. "Let's see if you really are my equal. Let's race down to Uruk. I'll even give you an advantage: I'll carry that gazelle over my shoulders. Give it to me, Enkidu."

Reluctantly, I gave away Splash. I caressed her head, hanging in a way so unlike her, kissed her hardened snout while he watched me with terrible quietness.

Ho, ho, hurrah! His company galloped off through the woods, and he bounded ahead before them. Wild ass on the run, I swung through the stranglers after him, leapt over cypress roots and dark cedar bogs, around the box-wood. But soon the pounding of hooves became dim, mist slavered from the earth. My legs grew stiff from running. At the thorn bushes, I lost the way. Loping up and down the thatch of shadows and across a stream, I tried to find the path of his horses. I could not see it. At last I curled up under a rock alone.

He will come back for me when he finds that I am lost.

But even as I had this thought, I felt such shame I had to bury my face in the dirt.

I stayed under that rock in the woodlands, lamenting my lost sister and my lost self, for too long. I was still there when I heard his *zamzams* celebrate his return, his *tigi* drums crash like the burning heart of a rock that falls from the sky.

Only after the fires of Uruk began to dance in the river and across his swaying date grove, casting a glow across the Valley of Sumer that penetrated the forest all up and down my side of the Zagrebs—only then did I hang my head and go searching for the way back up to my home.

When I came out of the woods, I thought the stars looked distant and self-absorbed. But didn't Silver Friend lean through the boughs of her dark tree to tell me, *Stop dragging your heels*? No. The moon sat crackling in my water hole, circled by a ring of rock. Steam rose from the nostrils of my gazelles as they chewed the sweet, colourless grass.

Up on my crag, the black rectangle of the trapper's door rested against Olive's trunk, as silent and mesmerizing as a future that reveals nothing. But you walk toward it, arms out. You begin to run. You beg it: *Please, if you are inevitable, do not make me wait.*

I called to my sister gazelles, "Don't you airheads know about the death of our sister?"

"Life is sharp," they said.

᠉᠊᠊᠊᠊᠊᠊

My door—I obsessed over it.

I began to fear the space behind it. No matter where you stand in relation to a door, there's always another side.

I did not roam the hills. I did not go with my herd. I lost the intuition of runners. If I scavenged for berries, I took my door along. I would hold it over my head and walk into its slab shadow. If I got too frightened, I dropped it flat on the ground and leapt on top of it, and then I would not want to lift it again, scared that if I swung it open, a room would appear, and up from the room Splash would come, stiff as whale skin, her eyes black pearls, a bloodless wound in her neck, complaining of thirst—but she is blind, she cannot swallow. And she would ask: *Why did you leave me down there alone when I want to be in the bright air that continues to surround my kin? I want to fall at the roots of a tree and for the tree to eat me.*

My sisters said, "Why do you sit? Your face is a lair."

"What is our destination?" I asked.

"Come, run through the grasses, play at the water hole."

But I did not want to splash at the water hole. I wanted to sit and pet my gazelles, whisper secrets into their tawny ears, secrets I didn't know I had, that I must have invented.

Before long, my sisters grew bored of my petting and ran from my touch. I stared into their black eyes. "I am here," I

14

said. "Here I am." But more and more they took off for the uplands and left me behind like the weakling at the back.

I sat down under my crag and wept so my mother could hear me.

"Humbaba, you gave me something I loved and took it away."

Behind me, far up, a gust of her auras called from the top of the world: "Eh, whiner, don't I got stuff to do?"

"Humbaba, I'm disappearing and it makes me afraid."

"That screaming eyeball who came—crows told me— what did he promise you in exchange for permission to hunt my children?"

"Existence, even when I'm not here."

"And what did you say to his offer?"

"I didn't tell him nothing, Humbaba."

"You lie."

"Humbaba, I didn't tell him nothing!"

"It's that flatness with no hands you're holding. Leave it in the woods, dealmaker. It's dead, so leave it in the woods."

"What, this old trapper door? It's just a game I like to do."

I hugged my door to my chest and waited for her to go back up the mountain.

"It's *mine*," I said, practising the tightness of that word.

❧

One night, returning from sweet grasses with my door in my arms, I came down into my place alone and discovered a woman standing at the edge of my water hole.

She wore the pelt of a white cow, slit up the middle. The cow's head, with its bored-out eyes, sat stacked on hers. Inside the slit hide she wore a crimson dress, a colour I'd never seen. When she let fall her sleeves, her grey hair swept over her breasts—a curtain she parted with a shrug. Her lips were thick, ready to drink. Her thighs fat and strong. Her belly had borne many children. Comedian of abundant charms, powerful delights.

"Well, there you are, beautiful God-man. More like God-beast! My, you make me laugh. I thought beasts couldn't cry, but here you are wailing down that mountain pass like a ghost. Baby-God, why is weeping the one human behaviour you've acquired so skilfully? Why not laughing, like me? Why not making promises? Why not baking clay into bricks and building a wall? I know exactly why not, God-man. I've got the answer for everything. When have I ever seen such magnificence abandoned to solitude? No wonder you're lonely and a monster—you've no dream to live in, just a colossus of pure energy. Even the Gods have a world to contain them."

She let fall her bangles from her wrists. She let fall her raiment from her hips.

Was it desire I felt? I'm ashamed to remember. With what relief I sank to my knees and crawled toward her!

With only the music of the silent stars, she began to dance, side to side, making a square with her hands. I slithered toward her.

"Closer," she said. "Closer, dog."

"Did Gilgamesh send you? What did he tell you about me?"

She laughed.

Dim, convoluted patterns had been tattooed onto her skin: a head, a foot, a water bird, a triangle, two wavy lines, a fish, a stalk of barley, a sun in the valley basin. On they went across her wide stomach, down the geyser of her navel, across the back of her hand. She stepped backwards and leaned against a rock, reached down into the mound of more hair, and showed me her sex.

"I am Shamhat the Holy, Harlot for the Dead. I have been sent by Gilgamesh to make you a baby. If you come back with me after our cavorting, you will be the only man in Uruk, other than him, to father your own child. He has never made such an offer before."

I fucked her like I'd died of thirst, and she was water at the site of a massacre. For days and days this went on, me leaping at her and trying to climb inside. Then, after every satisfaction, I returned to myself, disgusted, but it was a sweet disgust I wanted to keep near me and eat. Sometimes, over the course of those days, I watched her sleeping in the shadow of a rock and told myself, *It is done now—run away*. But always emptiness echoed across my heart, and I would crawl over to her at exactly the moment I most wanted to leave. Guiltily, I kissed the fat, rotten crook of her knee.

On the fifth night she said, "Gilgamesh sees you in dreams. You are a rock fallen from the sky and he cannot dislodge you. You are an axe in Uruk-the-Town-Square, and the crowds mill around you."

"He killed my sister."

Her sharp crow eyes loomed. "Gilgamesh has uncontainable angst. He makes the biggest men of Uruk fight each other to the death. He rapes all the pretty boys and girls. There is a bed in the centre of Uruk where he rapes all the new brides in order to father each and every one of Uruk's children. Why? To control the only thing that escapes his grasp: the future. Do you know what rape is? It's tearing out another person's mouth and using it to chew your food."

"So why don't you people smash his head with a rock and be done with it?"

She sighed. "You know very well why not, Enkidu. Did Gilgamesh not plant the date groves? Did he not dig the claypit and build the walls around Uruk with oven-fired bricks? Was he not the first to dig oases in the desert, the first to dive for coral? And is it not Gilgamesh who will harness radio waves, who will freeze dry milk and discover the apocalypse in a cracked atom? I tell you, Gilgamesh is the wisest and most magnificent of men. He made the world. Without him, Akkad would make Uruk a haunted place. Nippur would make Uruk a haunted place. The Amorites would say, *Breezes haunt your sheepfold, the lament has been made for you.* Look, he knows he is a savage, wild bull, addicted to the deep. But every time he drinks wine and eats hashish, his loneliness overtakes him and he loses all control. Then, when he's sober, his face is an expression of woe. He lies in a dark room brooding on death and asks, *Is anyone as lonely and terrible as me?* You like to play, don't you, Enkidu? Well, I've got a play for you. Act his equal. Absorb his energy. Get him to leave us alone. That's what he wants you to do."

"What about my mother, Humbaba?" I said. "She's bigger than even Gilgamesh. She's a terrible monster at the top of the world, tall as a cedar, with tusks down to the ground and a face like intestines. She mothers all the distinct species, seven a day, filling the world with variation. Even you people came from Humbaba. Appeal to her."

"Tusks?" Shamhat said. "Intestines for a face? Enkidu, you're talking about an elephant. Ah, you poor baby. If this elephant was our mother, we'd know it. She would take care of us."

My warmth drifted away from me then and, terrified by a roar of silence, I looked into Shamhat's wide, frenzied eyes.

"*She* knows!" I pointed at the full moon hanging over the water hole. "She's been listening to everything you say. She's laughing so hard she almost fell out of her tree!"

I bounded toward my water hole and leapt into Silver Friend's reflection. Under the water I watched particles of clay that sparkled like little pieces of silver that had fallen out of her hair when she scratched herself.

When I came up to breathe, Shamhat was staring at me with a sad expression.

"Who did you say that was? *Friend*? Oh, poor bear. Poor Baby-God. But how would you know what's what, living out here all on your own? Aren't you what I would be like, if no one taught me anything? It isn't wrong to think of the moon as your friend."

"Moon?"

"Yes, dear one. That is the moon. It is gentle. It waxes and wanes but never wanders far. This produces life in the heart. But if the moon turns against you, you'll be cursed with an Asag demon that makes you depressed."

Then Shamhat pointed up with a stick and taught me about the Igigi and the Annunaki, the planets in their aspects of love and death, and about the constellations of immobile stars. She taught me about human constellations as well. I learned about marriage, property, the potency of blood. About the order of the cult and the order of the state, superimposed upon one another, each with its own New Year Festival at the spring and autumn equinoxes. She taught me about the Land of the Dead.

Packed so full of knowledge, I lost the ability to speak from the heart. Even when Shamhat gave me her breast to suckle, it made no difference. Later, scavenging for berries, I discovered I could no longer leap through the air. And my gazelles! From across the water hole they stared at me with their silty eyes. I knew they wondered, *Why doesn't he go play at the water hole, run through the grasses?* How could I tell them I was no longer a child of silence, I had been adopted, and now I had another way of being close?

In the presence of animal cousins I'd known all my life, a new shyness came over me.

"This is always what it's like to make yourself intimate with a stranger," Shamhat sighed, when she saw this. "Enkidu is enhanced. Enkidu is diminished. I pity you, baby God-beast. But what can I say? Destiny is bigger than your home-felt delight."

Two days later I let her shave my back. I sat still as she braided my beard into a cable strong enough to pull a cart and clamped it with one of her brass bangles. When she told me, "You are groomed," I nodded meekly and followed her down from the uplands, into Uruk.

❧

Of the journey down, I remember only the change from grey to green, and an infinite rot in the cracks between so many things. News of my coming had spread through all the outlying villages, and crowds of green-eyed children gathered around us, banging on little drums. At the end of a straight highway, Uruk's brickwork rose before us.

Because I was a man obsessed with a cracked door, what I saw next swallowed my heart. The Seven-Barred Royal Gates towered over us, six cubits of solid bronze overlaid with huge-eyed golden faces. Two leaves hung on pivots from a bronze stile. It was a door like a mountain, but a child could push it open with one finger—a marvel to behold.

Old men and women fell to the ground and kissed my heels. In their fish stalls lining the road, young women screamed, "God-man, put a baby in my belly, to bring you water when you are dead!" All the green-eyed children dropped their drums and brought me bowls of milk.

"Drink," Shamhat said. "We're your mother now."

A crowd led me down the Street of the Gods along the Inanna Canal, past courtyard houses arranged by profession. At the end, Uruk-the-Town-Square revealed its convoluted ugliness. Tents and colourful lanterns, torches on high poles. Huge were the eyes and toes of the winged statues. Across their belts, and carved along the fine edge of brass censors smoking lemon and sage—on the walls of the ziggurats—row upon row of scribal art explained Uruk to itself, and bore it forward in time. Not that the wild lacks detail, not that I hadn't examined the veins of a leaf or watched a leech swell on my thigh for entire afternoons. But now minutiae screamed to be seen. Everywhere, I was afflicted by the ghost of a maker.

Behind the hands of dancing party girls and playboys rose the terraces of the House of Head in Heaven, half a square mile in magnitude. My heart merged with lyres beckoning to darkness, horns calling people home. Revellers drifted across the Pure Quay in boats punted by large, stony women. All the people, their hair half a cubit high off their heads in braided black coils, were worlds unto themselves. Everywhere I turned was a ledge off which I might fall into the dream of another person's life.

A gazebo made of red reeds rose from within a circle of a hundred torches. Over this house hung a canopy of skins: lions and gazelle, ibex and hyena, leopard, sheep. Around it, drunk, thrashed the best of men.

Golden Gilgamesh was dressed in the pelt of a gazelle. Head, legs, tail, hooves. All of her, the one I loved. He ran around hooded in the face of my sister. The holes where Splash's black eyes had been, so mischievous, bewildered his sight. Her snout covered his nose. But his teeth were his own, gleaming like stricken ivory under the torches.

He swung a wooden mallet and chased after a ball. Behind him he pulled a naked young man on a brass chain. That was the bridegroom. In the gazebo, on a mat of red reeds, a woman waited in a purple gown. Her dark eyes rolled back and forth, following the ball. In her hands she held a small vermillion pot.

When Gilgamesh saw me coming, he dropped the brass chain. The drummers fell silent. The bride fled the gazebo, her pot smashed on the stairs. She dragged her groom away, his chain trailing after them. Oil flowed out of her smashed pot, shiny and subtle.

Shamhat stepped between us in her tall white cow's pelt. "Gilgamesh, my son with the restless spirit. I took in the stench of this beast and made him a man for you."

He said, "So what? Each time another man's child is born, my fame dies an hour. If you have his baby, I'll eat it."

I ran around her like a devil wind. *Crack!* I seized Gilgamesh by the shoulders and slammed him into a post. Down we went in the bride's spilt oil. When I opened my eyes, my sister's face hung over me in the light and smoke, trailing his glittering beard of gems. Huge hands choked me. He roared in my face. I wrenched his white beard plait, blood gathered on his chin. I knocked his elbows, releasing his hands from my throat, rolled over, slammed my foot into the ground and tried to stand. He leapt up and threw me onto my back. My breath huffed away, blood warmed my lips. Around us the gazebo crashed to pieces, torches toppled.

Gilgamesh knelt above me, radiating like a star. The crowd heaved waves of eyes. Regarded by the one regarded by all, I'd never felt so real. I smiled at him.

Spreading his arms, he recited the lines he'd prepared for this moment. "Mighty Enkidu. There has never been a man like you, other than me. I sent you my own mother so you could put a baby in her. Your uniqueness and excellence has cured my desire to father all of Uruk's children so they might bring me water when I am dead. I will have enough water in the Land of the Dead for ten thousand years, and after that I'll have had my fill of death. Let other men live, for I have you. Now let us show the people a feat never before done in this land."

He took my battered face in his hands and kissed my mouth, bent and threw me over his shoulder, my hair trailing at his heels like a veil. I knew he relished my weight and the difficulty he endured as he carried me.

In his room lit with torches, I crawled on top of him, pressed my bloody nose to my sister's snout, petted her scalp, kissed her ears. He arched his back and yelped.

That man with no equal—all he wanted was to be at another man's mercy.

"Hurt me," he begged.

But I went gentle with oil from a *kor* next to us. I went slow. I pitied him.

Then, trapped on me, he fell into the pleasure of his anguish and I began to despise him. I tore my sister's pelt from his face. When he grabbed for it, humiliated without his mask, I made him scream. He could not escape.

Looking back, I think this is how I lost my beastliness and became a man. This war between pity and disgust.

꙳꙳꙳꙳

Twice the river flooded and dried up. Then came the season of Dumuzid the Dategrower, then the season of Akitu Cutting the Barley. I spent one year in Uruk.

With me, the city improved. This, I discovered, had been the great desire of his life, to find a friend to make him kind. Every day, supplicants arrived at the gates saying, "Let us into the great city of Gilgamesh, renowned for its justice, and we will bake your bread. Uruk is the world's tiara." The threshers sledged in peace, reed pullers rang little bells as they kept up embankments along the canals, green-eyed children skipped in the streets carrying gifts Gilgamesh had given them, brass dolls with wind-up springs. A digger in the pit earned a silver ring for every basket of clay. Who in Uruk wasn't rich?

In his gold paste and wearing a white gown of swan feathers, Gilgamesh paraded through his streets handing out dates to the women and men he used to humiliate. I followed him wherever he went, pasted in silver. I felt myself hardening under the people's attention, growing sharp, transparent, as if even my intimate desires would correspond to their dream of greatness. They did not know the thing I desired most was to become the person they thought they saw. But where was that glorious God? What did he want?

Shamhat had borne an olive-skinned, green-eyed daughter who looked exactly like Gilgamesh.

Privately, back in his room, Gilgamesh tried to brush this off. "Don't worry, Enkidu. It doesn't always work. The woman needs to be at her right time. The political purposes of that ceremony are accomplished and the child can still be your own. When she grows up she will lead the Ministry of the Exterior in your name. You can be proud."

"I'm empty," I complained. "All the world looks like a sad place. People suffer and seem depressed. I love you but I can't get near you. I'm always alone."

"Then play with me," Gilgamesh said. "Games are a great cure for loneliness. A nature like ours has two parts: the part that craves glory and the part that seeks a friend. Only in the game are both of these instincts satisfied! Come, join the frenzy, seek admiration—all your troubles will fly from your mind and you'll feel close to your own life again!"

But though I was more excellent than twelve human beings combined, I never once beat Gilgamesh at anything. Not wrestling, not mallet and ball, not orgies, not dance, not play-acting: in all of these he was a devil wind. I once merged with my throng of gazelles with delight in my heart, never losing the sharpness of my mind. Now each breezeless night I paused with a mouth puckered by wine and hashish to stare at the moon, the city's terraces rising so high they seemed to stab her.

"You were the good thing," I muttered.

Always the sound of drums, the flash of tools. Off in the distance, a dull terror hovered. That was the desert.

If I got too plaintive remembering my herd and my place and the moon, Gilgamesh frowned and pulled me aside to ask questions. What did I miss? Was his humour too caustic? Was humanity too broken? Had the purity of the wild been defiled?

"Tell me again why I'm the first one you ever loved."

"Enkidu, you are a man with no instruments and delight in his heart. Who but you exists so closely to his own life? You are as true as the first day of the world."

⇜⇝

He could not sleep. It is not good to lie beside your friend each night and watch him become a stranger as he moves through the dream place of his own mind. It was me he dreamed of—he mumbled my name. Where was he taking me? I didn't like the smallness of it. I was jealous of the tiny Enkidu he took on journeys while I stayed behind with no dreams.

Sometimes he spoke in that high, slow voice from his sleep: "Enkidu is on the river with an empty hook, eating salt. He says, 'In this nightmare I cannot move my arms!'"

In the dark one night, I wept next to him. "Where's my herd? Where's my mother? Where's my friend, the moon? Are you really all I've got?"

"I am a God," he said, fully awake. "Aren't I enough for you?"

He jumped up and went to his vanity, and stared into his reflection. Even he looked astonished as he scanned the deepening ridges, the stains rising in his irises, the solitary hairs coiling from his braid like the grey tails of pigs. He took a pot of gold paste and, with two fingers, plated himself. The room filled with the reek of animal fat and ground almonds.

"Am I so ugly?" he said.

I flew up and grabbed his precious beard. He opened his mouth. Then he stood and flung me to the floor. He pushed my head into the ground. I knew what it was to feel the carelessness of a God.

After, by the low light of his travelling brazier creaking along its track, he rubbed my shoulders in oil and begged me to remove the blankness from my face. When I didn't, he went on a rampage around the room, smashing pots. He pinched my nipples, tore dark hairs from my arms, fretted over me, massaged my feet.

"Aren't you wild and free of cares, Enkidu?"

"I live in an enormous city, but my experience shrinks. A bitter Asag demon has cursed me. When I look into a person's eyes, all I see is my black-bearded head."

"Even when you look into my eyes, Enkidu?"

"Especially then, because your eyes are the largest and brightest."

He watched me with so much bitterness I became afraid.

"Do it," he said.

"Do what?"

"Be wild. I want to see the original game."

Desperate, I leapt up and did what I thought he wanted. I put on my sister's pelt, galloped out his window onto his terrace and down the stone steps, into his orange grove. He chased me in the dark, hunted me down.

Back in bed later, I made my own repetitive demands.

"Tell me what I'm like, Gilgamesh."

"Be wild for me, Enkidu."

꒰꒰꒰ ꒱꒱꒱

To build a monument that would prove to myself that I existed, and make others know me not just as the moon reflecting Gilgamesh's radiance, I would have willingly turned myself into an eyeless and unfeeling stone. Oh yes, I would have exchanged myself for my monument.

"Once you take root here," he told me, "you will not feel lost in a void of reflections. Your wildness will return to you.

27

Once you take root here, you will stop trying to uproot me."

He sought in many ways to cure me.

First he tried to educate me, but education made me mute.

Then he tried to teach me a labour of skill. I chose masonry, and built stairways to nowhere.

One day we rode out onto the plain and shot a lion in the heart. This was the closest I came to feeling glad, because even though it was Gilgamesh's arrow in its heart, and Enkidu's just below, he let me have the head. I made a mask of it and mounted it on my head. When I did this, the people were afraid of me. I stood at my height with power streaming out of me, happy to see them cringe. But Gilgamesh hated my unkindness and took my mask away.

"You don't mean that," he said. "Not you."

He next decided that hedonism was the answer. All day we sat by his scented pools drinking wine, getting up only to play lawn games. He extended the New Year Festival indefinitely and work in the city stopped. Then, one day while playing mallet and ball in Uruk-the-Town-Square, I changed into a fish. As mallets swung in the heat over crimson tents, their shadows stretching like the spindly legs of starving horses, everything flipped inside out. The background leapt into the foreground, and I found myself floating in a thicker element.

Crack! The bright willow ball swam past my feet—Gilgamesh had scored the winning goal, but this didn't sting me in the way it usually did. The sun poured down relentlessly and burned colours away.

As if following signs along an underwater highway, I left the game to pursue two cracks in the wall, dragging my mallet at my heel. They led me down a narrow street to a low, crumbling gate. Next to it, set into the stone wall, was a battered door of bound river reeds. It hung by a single leather hinge.

A fiery aura appeared beside me.

"Enkidu, what are you doing?" it said. Gilgamesh's features drifted into alignment. His gold paste had sweated off his cheeks and his shoulders slumped like an old man's.

"I can't do it. I'm not in the game anymore. I'm on the wrong side. I cannot merge with the wind. I cannot leap in a frenzy. My mind always says, *You're not doing it. Do it. You're not doing it. Do it.*"

"When I first saw you frolicking with those gazelles in the mud, my heart leapt into my eyes," Gilgamesh said in a miserable voice. "I thought, this wild man will save my life. Enkidu, is anyone as lonely as we are? We are extraordinary, but in the end, we lie down with the lot. I wouldn't wish this double nature on anyone."

"But I never used to feel so lonely."

"If a person suffers Asag illness, grief for no reason, if a person has bitterness in his heart, we tell him to proclaim the exaltedness of his God. But a God-man finds no solace in his own exaltedness. The only thing is to find an equal. Since you came to Uruk, I have not felt contempt for anyone. But all you tell me is that you want to die. Now I'm the one who is dead."

Fear came upon me. He'd told me he wanted to show me that his glory and beauty and brilliance were tired illusions, he wanted me to see him in his nakedness, as if he had not been born a king. I would be the only one to see past his wondrous brightness—not even the Gods saw past it.

But what was he, to me, without all this? Because he was the best of men, his love flattered me, his friendship lifted me into greatness. Oh, I wanted to beat him at something, but what if I succeeded and discovered he was not the best of men—would I still be Enkidu?

His eyes swelled into two pools filled with me.

"I know you're thinking about leaving, Enkidu. But going home won't save you. The distance you feel since coming here is the distance all human beings feel when they are struck by the brevity and strangeness of life."

From my fishy world I said, "Take me to the claypit again, Gilgamesh?"

He frowned and shook his head.

"Why not?"

"You're becoming sophisticated, Enkidu. That place is all pain. Old rags, cracked pots—you can't get off your horse for all the bogs of human shit, skeletons of boiled birds. Why do you want to go to that wasteland of mine?"

"It makes me feel alive."

He sighed and nodded. "Come on," he said. "But I don't like to go, though I know very well I'm the one who built it."

⇒⋙⊱⊰⋘⇐

On a platform made of reeds jutting over the abyss, we stared into the pit so void it looked as if a planet had fallen into the earth. Teeming lines of people descended into darkness by ropes tied to posts around the rim. Empty baskets dwarfed their backs. All were shaved bald save for a black forelock that hung in their faces. Around the edge, peacock men in high black wigs made from the hair of those same pit slaves paced lazily with their bows cocked.

Gilgamesh shook his head. "I wanted to build a city the Gods would live in."

"Now you don't like it?"

He snickered. "Ambition is the midwife of eternity, without which I would be nothing, just a sigh on the wind."

"Like me, before you came and took me away."

"How big do you think Uruk can get?"

"As big as the world."

He clapped a hand on my shoulder. "As big as all the worlds observed by stars. Gods help me, I'm still excited by the dream of it, Enkidu. What can I do against this power of mine?"

"Let them go."

He smiled. Turning to his men, he bellowed, "Start a fire. Cook the slaves some fish and let them sit and eat. If they gather together to whisper among themselves, lower your eyes. My Enkidu lives outside of history. Today we join him beyond the law. Everybody plays."

"No, wait." I put my hand on his arm. "Let's you and I play first." I reached around for my bow and cocked an arrow at the pit, which was being devoured before our eyes by a continent of slaves. "The first of us to get to three."

"No, Enkidu."

I shot my arrow into the silent clay. A tiny, bald person fell from the rope it was holding and rolled into the narrowing funnel. Little faces turned toward us like flowers toward the sun.

"Ho, ho!" I shouted, and shot again.

Next to me Gilgamesh cocked his bow and shot, once, twice.

The pit started to wail with terror, shifting into a hundred thousand cringing backs.

Shouting, "Hurrah!" we cocked our bows, took aim, let fly. I watched my arrow arch over the pit, the people below hoping it would fly over, and then it dove, expertly, at the right moment, down into the far side. Squinting my eyes, I saw a tiny figure droop by its waist from a rope.

I turned to my friend. His arrow was still in his bow, cocked. Gilgamesh stood as if paralyzed. His eyes had tears but no lustre. His bright cheeks hung like drapes from his face.

"I won," I said.

He was silent.

I threw down my bow. "Am I so pathetic you had to let me win, like a child? You've made a city for Gods, but what have I done? I'm so ashamed, I hate when you look at me. I want to be alone with the beasts in the wild, I don't want anyone to know I exist if I can't accomplish anything like you have."

"I thought you were above ambition, Enkidu."

How could I tell him my ambition was the source of my love for him? I couldn't. I hid deep down in myself and sulked. From my anxiety and revulsion, the flat mystery of my door returned to me, like a giant bird come to lift me out of my disgust—with joy I remembered my desire to see the other side of it, my fear of what might lie behind it. I thought of it resting against Olive, the two of them grey and alone on a forlorn crag.

For the first time in my life, I had my own vision, like the ones I'd witnessed Gilgamesh having. There, in the heat, over the pit, a door rose before me, one so huge it hung from the sky across the Plain of Sumer and divided the wild from every city along the Euphrates. With what force of suggestion would such a door work, upon the souls of anyone who dared to knock on it? A door with no pole or pivot, huge enough to block out the sun, striking all who look upon it with the terror of vastness. Anyone who walked through that door would transform from a beast to a man, a man to a beast. Through this door I might come and go between his world and mine.

I gripped his huge golden shoulders.

"Gilgamesh, let me build a sacred door between my world and yours. I won't be gloomy if I can go back and forth. I'll visit you and you will visit me. Listen. Back where my mother lives, seven cedars crown a mountain, absorbing earth's envy and expelling it into the sky. Nothing alive is as old or as huge as those trees. They are so enormous, just one of them would make your city look like a fly whisk. My mother guards them, my mother the experimentalist who mates with everything. I cannot imagine any other tree that would make a door like the one I just saw in my dream."

"Enkidu, I brought you here and made you a man, but I want your heart to keep its wild innocence. Is that not a contradiction? But I'll fix it. Your mother will give you one of her trees, all right."

So that was it. We made a *hassinnu*-axe and a *pasu*-axe with a whole talent of bronze each, and our belts also each weighed a talent. Gilgamesh ignored the protests of his councillors, but he did agree to let me lead once we entered the wild, for—as they all said—I knew the wild's paths.

Soon, the night came when we went to bed early, Gilgamesh with his back to me.

We left for the Forest of Cedars at dawn.

꘎꘎꘎

It was as though I had no memory, to rediscover the sky on yellow hills. Up, up my legs took me, not as easily as before, but still, my thighs had lungs. I wish we could have climbed forever.

"Gilgamesh, the valley's fog has cleared. Don't your biceps have hearts?"

He turned his radiant beard back toward Uruk.

"The city wailed for me, didn't it, Enkidu? It said, *If Gilgamesh leaves, will Aratta make Uruk a haunted place?*"

"So what? All the cities of the world are haunted."

I hallooed to Old Olive gripping the night like a claw. Against her leaned my door. The moon hung half-full over my ring of crags. For a moment I forgot about the Gods and about the moon and saw Silver Friend's wide grin laughing down from the sky into her mirror. I ran into the cold silver centre of the water hole. I leapt and splashed, I spread my arms and waited for Friend to shower me with a thousand tiny seeds shaken from her bough.

Gilgamesh sat and observed me. He took a copper mirror from his pocket, examined his reflection with a scowl, and quickly reapplied his paste.

I scaled my crag—not as easily as I used to do—and brought down my door. It was paler than I remembered, and lighter in my hands. I laid it down in the mud and slept on top of it.

Gilgamesh woke whimpering in the middle of the night to tell me about his nightmare. "Don't you hold me anymore?" he said.

I put my hand on his back. "Hush. The place you go when you dream is smaller than this one," I murmured, massaging his neck.

But I wasn't one to talk. My magic door rose before the eye in my mind, hanging between the sky and the earth, on and on, the edges seeming to converge yet never touching, while a voice counted, *One, two, three, four.*

Watching him sleep with his back to me, I reasoned, *Who cares that my domain is unshaped by smoothness of thought? It has expanse!* It was the wild that reached to the cosmos, not Gilgamesh's sophisticated symbols of heaven.

In my fantasy, the awe of gods and goddesses shone back at me the braveness of my life. *With what force that door keeps people out!* cried the planets in my fantasy. No genius on earth other than this one could build a door like that. He needs no city, no wall—the audacity! And the godlike skill required, the might of this simple vision—a bare door, huge, hanging there. There's nothing on earth I'd rather look at!

Still clutching my door, I woke with a chill, covered in sweat. The silent dark made me embarrassed for the excitement of my thoughts. I climbed my crag and sat under Olive. I rested my head against her, reached up, and plucked her salty fruit.

"Olive," I said, softly knocking her. "Do you think my plan is good?"

But no wind came to make her speak to me. She just stood there, stiff and unconscious. And what about before? Had she never listened, when I rested my chin on her branches and said what bison I saw in the mist? Had she never accepted my thanks for her fruit, happy to give—or worse, did she feel nothing, sense nothing? Had Olive always been a dead thing? "If so, I should cut you down and make something useful out of you."

Looking out over the slopes that were so high and jagged, and the valley below—so humid that in my previous life I had never seen the fires of Uruk through the distance and the fog—I looked down at the trappers' humble door of cracked, grey wood, lying next to Gilgamesh. I felt, in my desolation, solace in the mystery of a presence abiding behind and pushing through, that weak geometry of inside and outside. Oh, I wanted to be a man. I wanted to want whatever it was men wanted.

In the morning, we ran up the pass toward Mounts Lebanon and Sirion. We ran faster than human beings, we ran east up seven mountains to Humbaba.

❧❧❧❀❦❦❦

Up on the glade at the pinnacle of the world, the sun sat atop the Canopy of Cedars like a Thunderbird in its nest. *Let me take away that fear in your heart,* the trees sighed. I hugged my door to my chest. Everywhere chimed with the music of those little bright birds who followed Humbaba around and delighted the world to play. Off in the distance, over the peaks of smaller mountains, silent lightning struck the slopes. Humbaba's laughter echoed off the underside of boughs.

With more delight than I had ever seen, Gilgamesh pointed at the festivals of flying monkeys and at the celebrations of squirrels careening across the canopy of green. Sap rained down into the open mouths of beasts. My friend looked so young!

In the wide green of the grove, between tree trunks so huge they were seven mountains on a mountain, Humbaba rolled in the soft needles and giggled as her seven sucklings clung to her teats. They each would have a suck, then all at the same time jump to the next teat. She lifted her creatures onto her tusks and slid them down. Bigger than human infants, Humbaba's children. One with the face of a cat and the body of an ape, one with a shell on its back, one with a long nose, one with claws for hanging, another without eyes, one which could already leap up on its mother and balance on the curved ends of her tusks, one which slept as it suckled—Humbaba moved that one herself in the whirligig.

Her seven vulvas still swelled from her labours. One on her back, one on each thigh, each shoulder, and two between her legs. In all seven wombs, new faces floated, new tails thrashed. Eternally pregnant, eternally nursing. Always she gave off the encouraging smell of iron.

"Ho, ho, Humbaba!"

She turned her huge head slowly. Chewed-up mushroom gills were stuck to her chin; she was always trying new things to eat. One of her eyes had swelled shut from the mushroom. The other leapt out from the wrinkled casing of its swollen socket, buck-naked and shameless. Her fleshy whiskers trailed like intestines down to her teats.

She said, "Why are you down like that, Little One?"

I had set down my door and was kneeling on it.

"Humbaba," I said, "mother of all species, seven a day, who mates with everything and fills the world with endless variation—"

"What, you come here to tell me about myself?" she snorted.

I looked up at her never-serious, terrifying expression, as she tickled her infants and poked at the fetuses. When had my mother given me the attention I needed? She did not see me the way I wished to be seen.

My eyes filled with tears for the lonely little beast raised on distraction.

"I came to introduce you to my friend, this great golden King with a radiant beard of gems dug up from the remotest parts of the earth. A cubit his stride, son of the Sky Gods, he found me and gave me my name: *Enkidu*. Now I am the one who saves him from his tyranny with my spirit of playfulness, and he loves me as a wife. But something terrible has happened. Mother, I am anxious all the time. I feel locked in myself, the world fades away. The city is killing me. But I cannot abandon Gilgamesh, who I love so much, or what will I have? So I am trapped, languishing, half-alive.

But then I discovered the power of doors, like this pale one I'm kneeling on. Listen to what a door is, Humbaba! On the one hand, they are nothing: mere suggestions, pieces of material, anyone could bust them apart. But on the other hand, they are what divide the inside of a person from the outside, his dream from the world. When you close a door behind you, you know that you are home."

She lifted me by my hair and set me down next to the door. She bent and sniffed it. In that light-serious tone she had, she said, "I told you to throw that skin into the woods."

I stretched my hand toward the youngest of the enormous cedars. When it tried to lift away my sadness, I resisted. When it tried to take my heart into the sky and relieve it of anxiety, I clutched on, as if anxiety was a possession.

"Humbaba, I'm talking about a door between worlds. Built from one of the tallest trees on earth, it hangs from the sky. It's what you'd call sacred, it exists as much in the mind as in reality—multiple domains at once! No pole or pivot, it hangs across the river valley with a gold stele on its front and terrifies with its vastness. With what force it would transform whoever walked through it."

Humbaba rolled her eye away. She got up with her sucklings still clinging to her and, like a ziggurat on a stone track built into the street, went about her business as if we'd already left. From one of her dark swollen slits, she squeezed a pellet of mud that she'd put there to staunch her blood, and crumbed it over the roots of one of her seven mountainous trees. The cedar ate the blood from Humbaba's wombs. She was their guardian.

"Humbaba," I continued with a feeling of hopelessness. "Walking through this door, a man could turn into a beast, a beast into a man."

"*Enkidu*, is it? Huh. I guess word travels slow up here. Well, tra la la. I'm older than you, *Enkidu*. I watched you from a distance when you were a baby. If a lion came, I chased it away. If a python crept up to you, I stood at my height. Now I'm thinking I should have hung you by your feet from a sapling. Looks like your life isn't enough for you. Now all you want is to live in your monuments."

"But don't you love me, Humbaba?"

She rose before us like a tidal wave. Her voice had a multitude of tiny voices in it; it made the noise of a carcass being devoured.

"I've loved you from the start of time. Yet the minute this King of eyeballs turned up and looked at you, all you cared about was, *What does he think of me*?"

"He knows himself!"

"Then why's he got to smear himself all over in gold? You two are a bad night."

Gilgamesh stood amid the drizzling sap like a shy baby. His bald head was anointed in sap, and hummingbirds hovered and pecked the sap that had collected in his ears. His eyes were two pits of embarrassment, his hands hung loose at his sides. Blinking, he looked at the needles that fell spiralling through the air to settle at his feet. A little goat with human hands crawled over and rammed Gilgamesh's shin, then sat back and rubbed her eyes. Gilgamesh's mouth twitched almost into a smile, but no. His face stayed only on the verge of relief. To what imaginary lands did my friend and I go to hide from relief?

"Humbaba," I persisted. "I know I'm asking you for something immense. But I am your son!"

Humbaba reached out her thumb and smeared my forehead with the mud of her womb. I felt power seep into me. Her power, and her disgust.

"There you go, Champion."

"It is a shame that you do not welcome your son," Gilgamesh said in a pitchy voice. "Especially given his glory. That is how to keep one's children away, though you have so many offspring perhaps you don't care anymore for your grown ones, like an animal. Enkidu's father must have been a great God descended from a cloud—only that would account for his superior form, his beauty, and his loyalty to his friends."

Above his head, Humbaba gathered like a storm. "His father was a whale's eyeball that washed up on the shore of the Gulf," she said with the low stillness of motion sucked out of the air.

One of her cattish infants ran back and forth along her shoulders, crying for milk and watching us with its unblinking orange eyes. My spineless brother. The little goat came and sat off to one side of Humbaba, nervously chewing on a long piece of root and fastening a cable of bunched grasses twitchily into her hair.

"My friend," Gilgamesh said, his green eyes rolling pathetically in his small head, "these trees are your inheritance. The project you propose of a door between worlds exceeds the limit of this chaos monster's imagination. If you want a tree, take it. The tree will not scream, *Don't take me*. The tree will not resist the bite of an axe. Do not give consciousness to inanimate things—that is the way of savages doomed to disappear into the soil of the earth, remembered by no one."

A terrible change took place as he spoke. It was Gilgamesh who changed before my eyes! The tyrannical destroyer, one third a man, one third a beast, one third a God.

Now, under Humbaba's angry shadow—in the atmosphere of her iron stench, under the orange eyes of her family circus, as the wind pressed with ancient silence upon the seven colossi dripping sap—Gilgamesh looked striving and small. He whined, he scowled, he sulked, and though still muscled and pasted in gems, he looked overblown. Under his belt I knew he had a paunch, from wine and dates and honeyed milk. His strength was only in his extremities.

I couldn't bear it. My fingers, clutching my axe, yearned to reach out. But who could have comforted me? My shame was too ambiguous. I did not even pity myself.

Deadly calm, Humbaba's face hardened, unyielding as a root. Fine grains appeared on her rigid cheeks, and her mouth was too still for a living creature. Her infants wept. My friend's eyes took in the terror of her auras. Gilgamesh squealed as a pig does when the slaughterer comes with his knife.

Humbaba gripped him by the throat, and it was like she grabbed my throat. I felt the awesome pinch. I felt the breath taken from me. Yeah, my mother was taking care of me, all right.

I swung my axe and hacked Humbaba's arm. Her mouth stretched into a terrible smile and her fingers froze wide apart in despair. Her babies turned over in her wombs. Her infants shrieked at the earthquake and clung to her harder.

As Gilgamesh fell from her grasp, I brought the axe down again on the vein in her huge thigh. Her face hung open in grief.

"All my work," she moaned.

"Forgive me, Humbaba," I cried.

Moaning as the blood left her veins, she leaned over her hacked thigh and held the still womb in her hands, the other wombs kicking. Her head of matted hair was bowed and her whiskers trailed in her blood. I raised my axe and swung it down on the back of my mother's neck. Then she multiplied, like maggots on a carcass, and each maggot was a man who lives in the mountains, each maggot was a woman who lives in the woods with her tribe.

With the void in my cheeks I screamed, "My friend, help me finish her, slay her, grind them all up so that I may survive!"

He came to my side and we cut down Humbaba's multiplication. Then, with our axes we took down the cedar, immortal and self-sustaining but eyeless and armless and helpless against our force. The mountains quaked, the white clouds turned black, Humbaba's auras ran screaming as we wrenched their infants from the strong grip of their arms. Dust rose. The beetles and worms that lived in the roots surged toward the sun's bright scream of annihilation.

Gilgamesh's reddened axe dripped with sap. He strode huge as a God through Humbaba's tiny, multiplying people. Through the tempest of fallen trees, he walked toward a tiny figure huddled near the head of a woman lying face down. It was a monkey, small as a toddler. It looked at me but saw no one.

I ran to Gilgamesh then, put a hand on his arm and stayed his axe.

What is to be done in a hurricane but wait it out? He and I, slaves to the hurricane, we waited for our storm to expire. Then, covered in blood, with desolation on our tongues, we stared past one another.

>>>><<<<

We sailed back to Uruk on a raft we launched down the Euphrates. Side by side, we watched smoke rise from the cut trees. To our raft we had attached the enormous lumber that tugged us down the river. Between us lay Humbaba's ivory tusks. We did not speak, we did not stop to sleep or to dream or to make an offering of flour to a hill. Already I was weakening. The chill bit into me, my sap ran away, the Gods turned against me.

We could not undo the curse. I lay in bed for two weeks, weakening with ignominy. I saw a tarantula come out of a crack in the wall. *I know the inscription on your door*, she tapped with the pads of her legs. *In the middle of the day, after a successful journey, the anxious shall stumble upon a temptation for brutality. Though brutality was far from their minds, their hearts will pound with excitement at the discovery that more is possible than they knew. Life will be seen for what it is, a dream. Force will carry them away.*

I did not go like a warrior in battle. But my friend stayed by my side.

Gilgamesh had not put on his gold paste for days, and now I saw his cheeks were liver-spotted. They hung from his face. His loose jowls: they hung from his face. His eyes, now empty of kohl, the skin around his eyes hung from his face!

He's ancient, I thought. *All this time he's been an old man.*

"Where are you, my friend?" I cried in the dark. "How did your radiance depart before my eyes? Humbaba, my mother, became like an enemy. I should have reached out and loved you for a man who was dying. But your frailty made me ashamed."

At that, I fell toward death.

After seven days, a maggot dropped from the nostril of Enkidu's beloved corpse. Only then did the knowledge come upon Gilgamesh that all his striving and ambition and tyranny and grief and petitions to the Gods amounted to nothing.

He tore the brightness from his beard, covered his arms in clay, and fled into the wild on a boat.

Look over the rim of your boat, Gilgamesh. This is what you most fear. It is the realm of the unborn. All your walls are in here, your valley has turned to dust. You are a crumbling mosaic in the desert, and soon a zealot will smash you. Kill the lion and his cub will grow skin. Kill the gazelle and her fawn will grow skin. Kill the ibex and her calf will grow skin. Reduce variation, bend the species to cure your anxiety, seek an elegant death in the wilderness. Love your idea. But, Gilgamesh. My friend, my love. The future will always have one up on you.

SO I CAN WIN, THE GALATRAX MUST DIE

THE GALATRAX IS A RARE WOODLAND CREATURE. The size of an otter, it has shiny, orbed eyes, a pugnacious black snout, and a short brown tail with a tuft of white hairs thrashing out the tip. It will swim, climb, and dig for grubs. Its most idiosyncratic features are its teeth. The long, pointed canines are in the front incisor position, not in the cuspid or fang area of the jaw. The French name for the galatrax is *petit morse*— little walrus. It can digest nearly any organic matter it finds: grass, lily pads, weevils, hornets' nests, carcasses at any stage of decomposition, scat. If desperate, it might pillage a nest. Like its distant relation the bear, it is a partial hibernator, sleeping in the hollow root system of a dead tree on a mattress of forbs, spruce needles, and milkweed for the months of January and February. The galatrax has the same predators as the muskrat, beaver, porcupine, and raccoon: these are coyote, wolf, lynx, and, if starving, fox.

Galatrae are beloved by culture. There is a popular series of picture books starring a quiet but bold family of galatrae, there are teddy galatrae, wall stencils of galatrae, and other paraphernalia. In clement seasons, galatrae will live close to humans, in the woodpiles outside of cottages. They adore the scent of warm spices; if you desire a sighting, make satchels filled with cloves and leave them about your garden. You may train a galatrax to take nuts from your hand.

Galatrax has a gamy taste. The meat is not as lean as chicken or bison, but only healthy nutrients saturate the blubber. Because the fat is nutritional, your body wishes to discard it. Remember: toxic fat is, in a classically tragic paradox, the hardest to lose. Your body is very attached to its pollutants. Even if you ate an infinite number of galatrae, your body, after digesting only the amount necessary to sustain life, will void the excess. Gorge all day: pounds will depart, muscles swell, veins protrude. Galatrax is one of the miraculous superfoods of our age.

Unfortunately, in order for the galatrax's beneficial properties to be actuated, it must be eaten raw, while living.

You sedate the galatrax first, of course, with a natural ginger compound. But if you're really serious, you may purchase a large glass hibernator to put in your kitchen, garage, or basement. The hibernator is a transparent cube with a sophisticated ventilation system on one side that lowers the temperature and oxygen content of the interior, while misting it with a steady stream of hydrogen sulphide. Do not keep more than fourteen galatrae in the hibernator at one time—enough for a week. Expect the area to smell vaguely of rotten eggs.

ᗐᗐᗐ ᗕᗕᗕ

The weightlifter does not want to think of herself as a person who devours two galatrae a day. She would, of course, prefer not to. She is as fond of galatrae as anybody else. But she doesn't indulge like this all the time. It is her pre-competition diet, which lasts only a month, and all the other weightlifters are eating galatrae, too. To abstain from galatrax is to lose. There is no need for citrus, vegetables, or water. Galatrax is completely sufficient on its own. And if she is regular and systematic—if she eats on a schedule rather than waiting to feel ready—it is much easier. First the workout, then the refuelling.

She is in front of her mirrors with her feet a metre apart, squatting in black underwear and a black sports bra. Arms in the air, a little jump, she grabs her bar and raises herself up and down forty times with full extension, ten reps with her legs down, ten with her knees up, ten with her legs straight out to activate the core and quadriceps, ten more with her feet crossed so she is not tempted to let herself drop.

She is panting, pacing her bamboo-click laminate. She puts a hand on her stomach and gropes at the superhuman hardness, which evades her—she cannot grab hold of anything—and she shakes her head with a sense of accomplishment that is strangely derealized yet not empty of gratitude—but for whom? It is gratitude in general. It comes out of her. We cannot know where it goes.

Two hundred lunges on each side, balancing a three-hundred-pound barbell on her shoulders. She bellows with lust, for her pain and her strength. There appears to be nothing in her mind but numbers. Ninety-eight, ninety-nine. Her neighbour on the other side of the duplex, if he didn't know her vocation, would think she was making love or being murdered, though it would be a very rhythmic murdering. She sometimes imagines, as she stares at her mirrors, that he might be on the other side with his ear against the wall, irritated, envious, or turned on—any of these possibilities console her.

Stiffly, the weightlifter deposits her barbell on its rack with all the slow, omnipotent power of a season. Her entire body screams for nourishment. Even her palms and feet are cramped with hunger.

❧❧❧ ❀❀❀

The galatrae are in her basement, asleep in their cold, deoxygenated cube. She does not hold the handrail as she descends the stairs because it forces her to rely on the strength of her thighs. Winning is just the inevitable result of a million micro-decisions.

She leaves the lights off. This is partially to immerse herself in darkness, though in fact it isn't very dark down here. A naive, watery rectangle of June evening spills through the window over the cube. Inside are ten fat brown-and-black balls huddled together, fringed by the white bushy tips of their tails, as if they are sleeping in snow.

It is best to see the low, furry hills of galatrae as a landscape of dollars. Two thousand in all: two hundred dollars per tenth of the pile. And yet, there is the smallest galatrax, the one with the birthmark. The arches of white fur across the back, connected by a point at the spine. A loopy *m*, like a child's drawing of a distant bird.

Earlier this morning, she swears, the birthmark had been three galatrae to the left. Yesterday, hadn't it been to the right of the centre? True, she is constantly changing the pile by removing one sleeping galatrax at a time. This was once a satisfyingly monotonous reduction of a unified mass, like bailing water out of a boat—but now the birthmark alters her perception. Suddenly the galatrae are individuals, organized around this outrageous sign.

She walks across her dark cement basement casually, as if she might be going to the freezer for a bag of pork chops. Near the glass cube, a few feet away from the window but still caught in the impenetrable column of clear, almost infantile light, is a laundry tub soiled with use. Having examined the tub's stains and notches, its old-fashioned knobs and the rust around the drain, the weightlifter has developed a theory that this was actually the builder's old sink, which he secretly took from his own home and installed here, while keeping for himself the new tub that should have been hers. The weightlifter is normally disgusted by the tub's filth, but in another frame of mind—particularly when she is starving—she knows she is flattered to be trusted with the secret of the builder's worst quality. And there is something else. The tub makes her ambition seem less bad. Even though it's just a tub, it's also an accomplice.

The weightlifter bends down in front of the hibernator and sticks her shaking hands into the plastic-lined armholes under the ventilation system. These allow her to handle the galatrae directly through a glove so that she does not oxygenate the case and rouse them. Normally, she simply takes the galatrax that is easiest to grab. But now there is this decision about whether or not to take the one with the birthmark.

Yesterday, the little galatrax with the mark on its back was not only the one nearest to her—it was also conveniently on its side, offering up its scruff for her to snatch. However, when she grabbed it, she was too gentle. She let her hand linger; it was not a grab at all. In fact, it was a stroke. And as instinctively as swatting a bug off a plate, she instead chose the galatrax next to it.

Each time she spares the birthmarked galatrax, it grows in magnitude. Where at first only one fourteenth of the mass had a mark, now one tenth has a mark. If this continues, the ratio will swell to one quarter, one half.

The weightlifter makes a deal with herself. The deal is that she will shut her eyes. Eyes shut, she waves her gloved arms around, carefully, to discombobulate herself without hitting any of the galatrae. Gently, she drags one of the pliant balls of fur into a little holding cell—a glass cube within a glass cube—and shuts the door of the inner receptacle. She removes her hands from the armholes, opens an exterior door, and lifts the chilled, soft body to her mouth. It is small, this one, under five pounds, about as small as a galatrax can get. She walks over to the laundry tub and bends over it.

As the weightlifter bites down on the galatrax's trachea, its eyes drift open and it twitches its long, awkward teeth. The weightlifter shakes her head back and forth to stun the galatrax so it knows it is dying. Its body, she has been told, will send a reprieve of hormones to dull the pain. Her mouth bites down but her hands are gentle. This is counter-intuitive and requires a great deal of control. With her left hand she holds the galatrax's head, and with her right arm she cradles its body.

The weightlifter rips open the galatrax's fur and fat and takes a large piece of it all in her mouth, plus some trachea. She chews as fast as possible. The galatrax is staring up at her almost lovingly, with half-mast eyes. It knows it is doomed and gives itself over. This is the total intimacy of prey for its devourer. They are soon to be incorporated.

Meanwhile the heart is flinging itself away from the chest. Before it stops, the weightlifter bites into the soft paunch under the rib cage. She thrashes her head back and forth. Her hands are not as gentle at this stage—it is too difficult to concentrate. Her face ravages the galatrax's lungs. She tears the tough blue lobes as they flap, forcing her mouth up under the diaphragm, her tongue instinctively seeking its way in the dark, and when it finds the spasming heart, she lunges, sharply, accurately as a viper. Her jaws are prepared to meet the small bones of the cardiac skeleton, but this one's heart is soft and easier to swallow—there are just a few ribbons of fibrous tissue, which means it is young. The meat is all things: acidic, bitter, and sweet, each flavour vague. It is perfect.

She lifts the creature up over her head and suckles the aorta. The carcass stiffens. The head sinks. The galatrax's snout rests on the bridge of her nose. Its two ludicrous fangs press against the skin under her eyes with the slow urgency possessed only by teeth. And now, as the fangs hang from her face, the weightlifter feels she is the galatrax. She scrunches her nose, an expert in navigating her face with these fangs, and experiences a painful kinship she will tell no one about. She loves these fuzzy innocents. We all do.

But there is also the fear these fangs inspire, one which we encounter only when another thing's dead matter—its hair, teeth, or nails—veers close to our faces. It is the fear that we are partially made of stone, we are inanimate. These fangs look too much like stalactites. At what point did stones become teeth? Even in fire and rock, the will gathers itself. She rests her face against the galatrax's and suckles the empty aorta.

She should rush to eat the organs while they still live, even though the galatrax is dead. Instead she lays it on its back over the drain. She takes a hook knife down from a shelf, opens the flesh between the rear legs and tears away the skin of the body. The pelt is inside out. She kneads the wet, veiny sac into a corner of the tub.

She uses her hands now to break the back, jerk the tailbone away from the spine, crack the legs apart, reach into the cavity, find the liver, kidneys, pancreas, ovaries, and pluck them out. She swallows them. She cups the galatrax's head in both hands and wiggles the skull until it cracks down the centre, leaving her with two distinct hemispheres sheathed in the tough but loosening scalp. She digs her thumbs through the chin up into the lower brain, and delicately nibbles the pulpy line all animals have under their noses and above their lips, as though their faces are made to be chopped in half. The head comes apart in two at the bottom. She sucks the warm, chalky coils out of each bowl, chews the thick, strange meat. It creams in her mouth as would a lightly cooked cheese. She sucks out the eyes, one from each piece of head, eats the lids and the black, fleshy snout, the rubbery lips. She bites off the vulva, tears away a hind leg and devours the meat, starting with the lacerated anus at the top. She funnels the intestines down her throat. They are long but thin enough to swallow whole if she doesn't panic. Now there is just the stomach, which tastes of bile, and some sacs filled with yellow pus. These are either glands or growths. She leans over the tub. Her eyes are shut, she is moaning, whimpering, chugging the frilled tripe, stamping her feet.

She turns on the tap. Quietly, with her face beside the stream of water, she inhales for a count of eight. The separate drops and smears flow together into a thick, oily river and disappear in tendrils down the gurgling hole. Fine cuts in the bottom of the tub—from the resistant claws of a pet as it was bathed?—have become packed over the years with a brownish sludge, so that looking down from this angle as she's doing now, the tub becomes a map of the Arctic. White plains, stone ridges. The drain a deep, magnetic mouth. She frequently draws romantic analogies like these. They make her feel close to nature. The weightlifter has never really stopped believing in magic, which is why, in her heart of hearts, eating these galatrae lacks a certain finality. Like most well-meaning but competitive people, she adheres to the idea that everything folds back into the one.

The weightlifter takes a towel down from a shelf and cleans off her arms, her face, and the front of her body. She wraps the bones, pelt and teeth in the wet, red towel. These she will take upstairs and throw in the compost.

She turns away from the tub and looks out at her dark, unfinished basement. Small brass frames glint at the other end of the room, where she rarely goes. Inside are paintings of horses, bugles, oaks, and men in plaid with hounds, in grasses. They could be old, these paintings that came with the house, as old as the tub.

Is it the June light or the niacin flush that makes the weightlifter appear strangely young? She already looked haggardly younger than her age, as pale, freckled people with thick, straw-coloured hair often do when they choose to wear heavy eyeliner.

One, two, three, four…nine galatrae are huddled together. She watches the slow undulations of their backs, the peaceful, resigned heaves. One mound over from the edge of the pile is a white wing. The birthmark rises and falls, passed over again. She holds both palms open at her breast. Slowly, she extends her arms.

⇝⇜

Upstairs, the weightlifter puts on a sundress and some sandals. She takes her compost outside to the green bin at the curb. As with many June dusks, the light is nostalgic. It fires the salmon brick of her duplex and drenches the cars returning home from work with a paleness that feels like another generation's coherence. This is a normal day in her pre-competition life.

As she turns to walk back up her driveway, her neighbour comes out of his half of the duplex. He is also taking his compost to the road.

The weightlifter, we've observed, is habitually careful. She knows that just because she and her neighbour take their compost out at the same time every week, this does not mean they are soulmates. It is six o'clock on the evening before garbage day.

"Looking good!" Her neighbour, whose name is Neil, gives her a thumbs up.

"If you ever need help moving furniture, you know where to find me," she replies.

She blushes and looks away. Possibly she's afraid Neil will think that by offering to help him move furniture, she's implying she doesn't care whether or not he moves away. People in love do tend to rehash every little thing they say for paranoid evidence of self-sabotage, even one second after they say it.

Neil is not particularly fit, more an arty type. But he does work as hard as she does. All day and all night, every day and night, the two of them dedicate themselves to their ambitions across the wall of their duplex.

"Lots of smoke on the horizon," Neil says. "For some obscure and stupid reason, it makes me want to have a baby."

They watch the distant smoke together.

Just then, a girl from down the street rides by on her bike, dinging her bell.

"Keep your eyes on the road!" the weightlifter says, but she is smiling—only wait, hold on. Well, all right. This is hard to believe, but the girl and the weightlifter are wearing the same dress, a red-and-white baby doll with an elastic cinch at the waist. It's a bad dress for bike riding. It hangs over the girl's feet so she has to pedal through the fabric. The lower half of her body resembles a globular mass, not like a creature or a monster, but, rather, a process that engulfs debris. Look at her go down the middle of the street, past all the houses, through the stop signs. Good God, without slowing down.

THE FUR TRADER'S DAUGHTER

My father, Hephaestus Rolf Knox, was a trapper and a taxidermist. He said that when he made me, he had formed my personality, as all fathers do with their children, based on a thought he was brooding on at the moment. That thought was: *if she's bad, I can melt her back down into wax, for I am alone as hydrogen, and as plenteous in my power, and no one can stop me whatever I decide to do.* When my father caught himself thinking this, he became angry. He'd wanted to make a daughter he could trust by imbuing her with compassionate, loving thoughts—and now he could never trust me. But I am pleased he thought it. That's the thought that gave me patience.

For many years, he and I lived on a lake in the woods. There, all we knew of time was the sight of the sun rising and falling over a ridge of cedar across the water. That, and a stopped pocket watch my father kept on the mantle.

Once a month we journeyed into the city for provisions. The city was an old woman with a million eyes. When we walked through her grey, cobbled streets dragging suitcases glutted on pelts and the stiff heads of beasts, I sought out light through the smooth towers of windows soaring over us. "Open your curtains," I said. "Open your eyes." "Shut up," Father said. "Stop treating the city like it's alive or I'll reduce you into a giant candlestick." But this is something I liked to see, at the time, and still do. Sources of light. And the city does feel alive because it is bright, it moves, and it will never leave its childhood behind, no matter how hard it tries.

Our shopping list was always the same: Arrow T-55 staples, non-putrefying wax, shoemaker's thread, surgeon's needles, wadding, newspaper, Plaster of Paris, arsenical soap powder, flour for Father's waffles, artificial eyes.

Day or night, the market never closed. Hundreds of stalls sat under grey paper lanterns strung between rooftops so thickly they made an artificial sky that kept out the rain. At our stall, we sold the usual savage icons craved, my father said, by a certain kind of suburbanite, like wild boar tusk and polar bear grizzle; but mainly our customers wanted softer fare, items imparting luck or wisdom, specifically rabbit foot or wood owl. If they liked to pretend they came from another time and place, they bought martin tail and ermine snout. Women talked about plucking their brows fine and buying red lipstick to go with their new muffs. We sold more than enough to get by.

I watched people in the market and they watched me. Most of them were city people, unlike my father and me, who had travelled from across a wide space. "Infants and their transitional objects," my father sneered, rubbing his hands together. He tapped his nose mysteriously. "When these cyborgs get bored of those little safety boxes in their pockets, that's when they come to us."

Other traders hawked beige lampshades printed with purple half-moons, underwear that said *You'll Love Me for Lunch*, bowls of addictive bagged puffs people could eat all they wanted of and never gain a pound. There was a man who sold "udderless cheese" made from pig milk, and a family that traded in dragonfruit. Every time we went to the city, my father had a dragonfruit, and each time he squinted as if in pain and said, "How can something so beautiful taste like nothing?"

Sometimes my father struck up a few words with the Algerian baker, usually regarding something lovely and impractical the baker's wife had purchased. "Narwhal figurines carved from narwhal horns, Hephaestus," the baker once said to him, "and little elephants made of ivory. She shows her ivory elephants to our customers just to see them squirm. 'Beautiful creatures,' she says. 'So beautiful.' And you know what? They're so uncomfortable, they buy the biggest box of dainties—but they never come back. You know what we are? We're a one-night stand!"

Friendship interested me most. I watched shoppers hold hands, brush shoulders, laugh at each other's jokes. None of them came near where I stood because they were afraid of the bees that hovered around my cloak. Still, I overheard.

She doesn't look real.

Did you see her skin has that grafted look?

She has to walk behind him.

It's like she's his slave.

Does he lock her up? Did he burn her?

"Hey, you," my father would say over his shoulder, if he also heard them. "Keep your chin down and don't look at anyone. Don't give them a reason to look at you. I am the law."

"*I* am the law."

"You're a walking, talking bar of soap."

I spoke to no one but him. My father bartered with potential clients, and I counted out their change, bagged their boar, antler, or bear claw, and kept my eyes on their pockets.

At home, when he felt fond, Father called me Little Buff Duck. But because I was always the same—obedient, quiet unless repetitive or recitative, and inexpressive—I could never predict when or why he'd experience a surge of affection. I did not like it when he called me Little Buff Duck. Both of us knew I didn't really have a name, and it was sad—very sad and pathetic—to pretend that I did.

$$\mathbf{\gg\!\!\!\succ\!\!\prec\!\!\!\ll}$$

He told me taxidermy was like eating liver: some like it, some don't, because even though livers are healthy to eat, they're nervous.

"That's why people avoid me," he said. "The taxidermy."

Really, my father was ashamed of his hideous feet. He attributed much of his unhappiness to them. He never mentioned them directly. It was safer to blame taxidermy.

Every night after supper I would ask, "Do you want the vanilla oil for your feet, Father?"

And every night he would press his palms together and say, "What I want is someone who understands me, and loves me, and who will not make me feel ugly, because, believe it or not, I too am a child of God."

Once, hot-eyed, he held himself erect in his chair and tapped my head with a hardened eagle claw glued to a stick. "If you became the queen of the world, I'd never bow down to you. I want you to know that."

I took the measuring tape out of my pocket. "Today your toenails are three quarters of a centimetre thick." I poked them with my needle-nosed pliers, which I kept on a string around my neck. "This sediment of dead skin is pushing your nail off. Oh, here it is. I have removed it."

"And I would *never* buy my child a car. Buy your own car! Buy your own pony!"

"I know your feet are hot, but you must sleep with your socks on or the oil will rub off on the sheets and your sores won't heal."

"It's because of the *taxidermy*, Buff Duck. It would take a rare lady indeed to see past its ugliness."

༈ ⤜⤜

During one December's journey into town, he caught a bug. My father's immunity had always been bad, because so many of its resources were spent staving off foot infections.

By the time we'd set up our stall, yellow shit hissed from the bottom of his trousers, and he'd wrapped himself in some now-unsellable lynx pelts. I watched his mess melting the snow but didn't know whether I found it repulsive or not. I could never decide what attracted or revolted me. I always went back and forth between the two feelings.

"Don't stare, what kind of daughter are you? Pervert." He shivered on a stool and watched me as if I were a fawn refusing to come to the dead mother he'd used to bait a trap. "You don't care. When I made you, I should have used more of my own soul." He coughed. "I should have felt love."

"Did you mean to spit that clot on your shoe, or were you aiming for the ground?"

He grabbed my arm, even though it cost him all his effort. "Get me some medicine. There and back, nowhere else."

He watched me as I went.

My face passed over windowpanes that revealed nothing. Two dazed and starving drones clung to the back of my hood. I searched those ancient, ground-level houses for vengeful emanations sucking air from cracks of broken things. Twenty million dollars a house. Across the street, a boy wearing a plastic Roman helmet pulled on his mother's hand, pointed in my direction, and waved a pamphlet that advertised nightly ghost tours.

Down a busy back lane between two skyscrapers, the apothecary knelt snug next to a shop where tourists could buy imitation medieval swords. Little bells jangled over the apothecary's door. I braced myself for a surge of warmth, but instead the room was cool and dim. Air seeped through cracks in the floor, making it seem as if the whole shop was elevated on stilts, as high as the sky.

The only other patron was an old woman who wandered across the front counter examining lineament creams. She found a blood pressure monitor and began testing herself. "This isn't right," she said.

"Can I help you?"

Although he sat behind the register, I hadn't seen the tall, elfin man until he spoke. He had a small pale mouth that reminded me of somewhere I might fold myself away and sleep. A tawny mole cheered his neck, and I moved between it and his lips while the old woman repeated her blood pressure out loud.

"Medicine," I said. "For a man."

"What kind of man?"

I considered. "A greedy man."

"Aren't we all?" He smiled at his apron strings as he tied them into a bow at the front of his waist. "And does he have the flu?"

I nodded.

"Thought so." He tapped a finger to his head. "There's a virus going around. I've smelled it; I can smell it on you."

He stood and went around a first, a second, then a third counter. Each one was higher than the last, making a warren of ledges and shelves that were connected at parallel, perpendicular, even acute angles. Time flowed in eddies that swirled in a cool circuit, losing and finding itself again. No one grabbed the back of my head, pointed my nose at a triggered leghold trap, and said, *Is there anything in there, Little Buff Duck?*

The old woman prowled closer and pretended to read the ingredients on a packet of lozenges. She cleared her throat a number of times.

When the pharmacist returned, he was holding a plastic vial of iridescent foam. "If he puts this up his bottom, it'll work in a jiff."

This struck me as interesting, and I said so. "I like the measurement *jiff*."

Laughing politely, he put the vial in a little brown bag. Only when he bent to press my change into my hand and saw the smooth absence of lines in my palm, and felt—I knew it—my candlestick density, my coldness, did he look into my face. He flushed and made a little O with his mouth.

"Are you for real?" he whispered.

"I don't know," I whispered back.

He slid his thumb under the coin and made little soft circles on my palm. "Can you feel this?"

The woman by the blood pressure machine leaned over, bumping her shoulder into mine. "She can't feel it. I can't feel it. Does it look like she can feel?"

I took back my hand and walked out.

Later, after my father had put the vial up his bottom and recovered with miraculous speed, and after we had made our way back to our house on the lake, I stared at my palm.

In the divot where the pharmacist's thumb had been, I found a thin, smooth line, like a kitten's claw mark. Inside of me, deep inside, I thought I felt something jump. I put my hand on my chest. "Come back. You *jiff.*"

The pharmacist's eyes were the watery colour of shore pebbles.

My eyes had no colour, until I mixed ash into round discs of wax and fastened them on.

ᔓᔔᔕᔖᔗ

A few weeks later, my father married the Algerian baker's wife, a German woman named Ilse. She was long and beautiful in a flat, angular way, and he adored her.

I could understand his loneliness, but his sudden ingratiation to this old-world woman confused me.

"What about the wilderness?" I asked him as we stood in the little white chapel with a flashing pink cross over its door, waiting for the justice of the peace.

"Shut up."

"What about the woods?"

"Don't worry, girlie. I love the woods," Ilse said.

"Has she seen your feet?"

My father kicked me, but just a little. He was on his best behaviour.

"Your ears are red."

"If your father has a wound, I would enjoy dressing it," Ilse said. "I would enjoy extracting the pus."

My father looked quietly at the floor. "There's no pus." He rubbed tears from his dark little eyes.

"You filthy, filthy man," Ilse cooed. "I love everything about you."

My father stole her from his friend with promises of fur. The baker had tried to win her back with her favourite delectations—ladyfingers, baby delights, grand-mère's thumbs—but she preferred the furs. She loved browns the best: beaver, muskrat, and fox caught between summer and fall.

Our living room became so cluttered with mirrors that it began to look like a lady's boudoir from a Schauinsland fantasy. She delighted in finding new combinations of fur, and I think even convinced herself that, though she lived apart from everything here in the woods, she was a stylist. She draped her torso with back and her waist with torso, made little hats out of beaver teeth, and framed the straight bones of her jaw with frenetically combed mink wraps. My father trapped, I preserved, and she brushed the dressed fur, braiding and unbraiding it.

A week after their wedding, she waltzed into the skinning shed wearing a wolverine tail. My father was on his stool, watching me flip deers' ears inside out. She stroked a dry patch on his neck and sighed. "One day, I want you to make me another like this weird girl. Only I want mine to play music. You know, like a box. And I'd like you to give her a more realistic body, not just a rectangle with legs and arms sticking out, and a head. Not that I don't think you're cute, girlie."

She winked at me.

He looked up at her. "Ilse, you shouldn't be in here without a mask."

"But no mask for Hephaestus?"

He took more pleasure in this, her asking him about wearing a mask, than in anything I'd ever seen. "Well, I'm used to all the chemicals, I know if I'm in danger." He tapped his nose shyly, grinning at his knees and scuffing his boots into bloody wood shavings.

⇶⫷

Our fixed-frame hives stood along the back treeline, amongst the sunflowers we'd seeded at random to attract the bees. Those hives brought me comfort. As it was from these hives that he'd harvested the wax to create me, it wasn't strange that I'd think of those bees as my oblivious, slavish mothers. Sometimes, when the days were long and I'd finished all the tasks he'd set out for me, I stood among the hives. If I stood there long enough, a battalion of bees would land on my head and make little hexagons on my cheeks. I felt proud to walk around with my hexagons, but my father would say, "Smooth that out. You look like a pockmarked teenager."

In April, bears travelled from lea to forest to lake, sucking grubs out of mulch and indulging in a sublime wanderlust. At least one bear per season lingered around the honey for too long. My father called these bears Winnies, and he said they yielded the nicest fur.

On the rarest day, a mother and her two cubs came for our honey.

That morning, I'd salted and stretched two muskrat pelts, warmed some red berry compote, and whisked the batter my father and Ilse liked to spoon into our electric waffle maker. He spooned hers and she spooned his. They wanted me to make the batter but I couldn't partake in the fun of spooning.

As I set the table, Ilse yawned out of their bedroom wearing one of my father's winter parkas and nothing else. She draped herself over my shoulder and linked one of her feet through my calves. "Are you joining us for breakfast?" She scraped batter off the side of the bowl and suckled it from under her nail.

My father came up behind her, washed, combed, and boyish. "I told you, Ilse. She doesn't eat."

I stepped outside and found myself truly unwatched for the first time in my life. Not even on their honeymoon had they let me outside, out of their sight; they had me row them around the lake, or sit in my room with the door locked. But more and more, Ilse was dividing my father's attention, if just a bit. Now he was only able to notice most of me. A part had become mine, to do with what I pleased. So I went to see the bees.

Spotlights riddled through gaps in stagnant clouds. I wandered among the hives, letting bees make hexagons on my cheeks, and went over to play a make-believe game in *Polynesia*, a sculpture my father had made along the property line.

He'd buried some trees upside down and hung moss balls from the roots with long strings. You never hear tree roots but they are frantic and they scream. Prancing on the moss balls and in the naked roots were a dozen chipmunks I'd drowned and stuffed, and dressed in petticoats I'd sewn from old ski jackets I found in a box in the basement. At first, I put my dolls in *Polynesia* because he let me keep them there when I wasn't playing with them; later, he said I must not remove them, because although Ilse found them cute, she hated seeing one on the stairs.

We like to sing about our little heads. It goes like this. Once we stuffed our mouths with butterflies. Their legs hung out and twitched. You thought we wanted nuts. Double whiskers for us!

I watched a duck floating on the water down by the dock. She was hiding from a mallard, which skimmed back and forth a few feet off, squawking for her. Silver eyes like hers would fetch a price if they were artificial. A generation of mushrooms fornicated through the grass at my feet with brainless pleasure. "The exquisite anguish of the fungus," my father said whenever there was a mushroom on his fork. On the mauve deck at the front of the house, I could hear my father and Ilse drinking Pimms.

Past *Polynesia*'s swaying balls, three shapes emerged from the border of the trees. Soon, a trio of black, fuzzy heads poked their noses into our clearing. The mother licked her snout. Her male cub swatted his rumbling stomach and nipped her on the elbow, egging her on, while the other cub, a female, tilted her head to one side, swivelling her antenna ears and listening to the silence of my heart.

After that, the bears came three or four times a week. I would have shot them if my father had told me to, but he didn't, he was so busy with Ilse indoors. So instead I watched them play. The cubs took turns climbing trees and diving onto their mother, who would respond by rearing onto her hind legs and sending the diver spinning. This went on until the surrounding bramble looked wallpapered with snagged tufts of fur.

Each visit, they came further and further into our clearing, until one day they stood just a few feet from the hives, waiting to see what I would do.

I broke off three pieces of honeycomb and tossed them over. "Alms for the poor. Alms for the poor, m'dears."

The girl cub cantered over to me. I took out a frame, scraped out the wax, made a ball, pressed it into my nose, and moulded myself a snout. I stuck two fingers in it for nostrils.

"Grrrrr," I growled.

The cub snapped at distraught bees, hanging her head near the ground and swinging it back and forth. She licked the honey off my palm. I scratched the divot between her eyes. She nibbled my thumb. When she got bored, she ran back to her brother and bit him in the butt. He peed on her. Their mother sucked on a piece of comb.

It was the nicest thing that had ever happened to me.

Suddenly, three shots warped everything.

My father floated out from behind a stack of firewood piled beside the house. Ilse followed in a black-and-white badger scarf.

"We've been watching you," he said.

"Like a chunk of beef under a deadfall," she said. "Cute though, girlie. You know I find you cute."

"I never knew you could get so friendly with anything," Father said. "It's been fascinating to observe."

My cub had been shot in the leg. She lay on the ground next to her mother and brother, licking her nose.

Ilse clapped her hands. She strode between carcasses, bending and sniffing, holding back her hair. "You have to skin them now, cutie pie, before they go sour. Oh, it's a shame, though. Such cute faces!"

My cub watched the woods, slowly blinking.

"Ilse wants a bear rug in front of the fireplace."

"And two little bear slippers. Because," she sighed, "if we kill them we should use all of them, every little skin and bone."

Father threw his skinning knife at my feet.

"Go," he said. "Start with the little one. That one there."

As I knelt down, I cupped her head and ran my fingers over her nose, so she would know that I loved her.

❧⟫⟩⟩⟨⟨⟨❧

My father's workshop had always seemed more real to me than the house. The labour that allowed the pretty house to exist took place in that ugly, dirty workshop, as if the mauve house—with its thatched grey roof and latticed windows—were the workshop's dream.

Usually I liked my father's workshop, because it felt like being inside a brain. But that evening, I hated it.

I flicked on the bulb hanging from a black wire, and then I lit the double boiler under the iron vat where my father melted his wax. The mother bear's pelt floated in the tanning tub at the back of the room.

My father said I wasn't alive because I didn't emit light.

"Light *and* motion," he said. "You've just got motion."

It is true my eyes do not glint and my tongue does not shine and the only colours I can see are black, brown, pink, purple, grey, and red. But I do respond to heat, which is a weaker kind of light. Every time I sew up the skin of an animal, I stitch its light into myself.

Behind the vat, on a shelf next to our square tub of arsenical soap powder, sat a crate where my father stored all the wooden moulds he'd used to make me. My father had carved the blocks himself. "I designed you to work hard, and not to fall over, and not to run away," my father often said, nodding to himself. "I'm a pragmatist, Little Buff Duck, and a man. Men plan. Everything they do has a point. So if you ever worry that you aren't beautiful, know you're beautiful to me because you work."

There was one extra piece of moulding, which I'd always known about but had never questioned. It was of a breast. It was made of a slightly different wood from the others, a bit of wormy maple, and looked like a solid cube with an oval dug out of the centre. I never knew which he'd made first, all the other parts of me, or that one breast mould. I knew it was a bad mould, because I had no breasts. It had never been used on anything, as far as I knew, and he'd never talked about it.

"No one has ever loved me," I said, which is something I'd often heard Father say. I liked to walk around with my hand on my forehead repeating it.

I warmed my face briefly with the torch. Standing in front of a little girl's mirror, I deepened my eyelids with a flat buck knife, straightened my jaw, and gave myself a pretty nose. I don't know where my father got the little girl's mirror. It had been there all my life, and seemed to come from the same place as the box of ski jackets I'd used to make my chipmunks petticoats. On the mirror's cherrywood frame, someone's mother had painted little bunches of pink and purple flowers. At the top of the mirror were messages written in lipstick, which my father had never bothered to wash off. *Hey, luv ya! Here's a picture of me so you can remember how ugly I am!*

I moulded two breasts for myself, and while they were still a bit warm, I took off my plaid smock, heated my chest with the torch, and stuck them on. I lay down on the bloody wood chips and waited until they hardened, watching myself in the mirror.

Now I will bring them a snack, I thought.

My father and Ilse sat silently at their game of Boggle as I came in the house. When I set down their bowl of nuts on the coffee table, Ilse's mouth twitched as if she wanted to laugh but wasn't allowed.

My father erupted off the couch, grabbed my hips, and plowed me down the hall. "What the hell are you doing?"

He pressed me into the wall. "Suddenly playful, are you?"

The oily bald patch on his head reminded me of a rabbit two hours after dying. Shoving me into the bathroom, he grabbed my shoulders and pushed me over the sink toward the mirror, which was large and framed by bits of calcified fungus.

Ilse's face smiled back at us—but a more serene version, with no lines. My breasts were perfect, taut, medium-sized: the breasts of his fantasy because they came from the mould he had made himself. He stared at me in the mirror, flaring his nostrils.

"Don't hurt her," Ilse said from the doorway. "Hephaestus. Obviously she's bored and needs someone to play with. Why don't you make another girl? But this time, make her for sweetness. Give her a music box for a heart. With her, there will be chiming and prettiness."

"I'm going to throw you both in a sack and drown you in the lake," I said.

My father snickered. "Not likely, considering you've just alerted us to your true feelings. You want a sweet new girl, Ilse, I'll make you a sweet new girl. But we've got to watch out for this one. From here on in, she's just for chores, not for daughtering."

He dragged me to the workshop. Slamming me against the wall by my neck, which he had designed to be very narrow and easy to grab, he reached up and rifled through the crate for my face mould. 'He pulled me to the workbench. As he pushed my face into the wooden box, the edges of it shaved coils of wax from Ilse's high cheekbones, which gathered at my ears. He clamped the mould shut at the back of my neck.

The flimsy walls shook. Through the box on my head, I heard metal and plastic things fall. He grabbed my hair, which that day was a weave of squirrel tails, and reefed me toward the vat, still warm from my work with the breasts. He stepped on my massive left foot, so I was pinned to the spot, and forced my head down toward the pale bog of melted wax.

"*Father* was never the right name for me." He snatched a metal ladle off a hook. "Maybe things would have been different if you'd called me *Master*."

He pressed the ladle into my neck and pushed my head under the hot wax. I felt my face rise and fall into its familiar shape.

When he lifted me back up and took the mould off, I saw that our tub of arsenical soap powder on the shelf over the vat was lying on its side, empty. It must have fallen over during the scrum and mixed its contents with the hot wax. I knew arsenic was bad for him, because my father always made me use it to treat the skins. If he ever used it, he wore his mask, which now hung from a nail in the corner like a magnified spider head covered in dust.

I was about to tell him about the arsenical powder when, raising my arm, I noticed I still had breasts. "What about these, Father? Shall I get the saw?"

He pushed me onto my stool and looked down his round nose at my breasts. His little dark eyes were like marbles. "I was right never to trust you. Ilse wants her own wax girl and we're going to make her one. She'll be my real daughter, mine and Ilse's. Go to sleep now. I don't want you looking at me while I work."

⇒⇒⇒⋅⋅⋅⇐⇐⇐

At dawn, I was not surprised to find myself still on my stool, with fishing line wrapped around my arms.

They stood in the cool, happy dimness of the work-shop, angrily whispering to each other. Ilse held a dress by its shoulders. It had a floppy crocheted collar and was probably a buttercup yellow or mint green or robin's egg blue, because to me it looked a washed-out red. My father knelt by the vat with the ladle in his mouth, putting on gloves.

New moulds cut out of Styrofoam were arranged in a body shape on the floor. Beside the head mould sat a little cardboard box with something shiny inside.

Now is the time to tell them about the arsenical soap powder, I thought. But then I decided not to. I wanted to see if his hands would burn off, even with gloves. Then he might make new hands out of wax, and we would both have wax hands, I thought. I was very happy.

Starting with the foot moulds, Father dipped and ladled in a smooth, wide motion, as if swinging a weight back and forth on a string. Behind Ilse, two grey satin slippers a third the size of my feet sat on the workbench with their toes touching. I only wore shoes when we went to town, and only to appear normal. My shoes didn't even have soles because I had a hard time navigating the ground through an extra layer of rubber.

Would this new girl feel lost in her slippers?

He hung the feet moulds from some hooks on a metal bar, and from there moved onto the long, shapely legs, the slim torso, the arms, hands, elegant neck, and finally to the face and head. Afterwards, triumphant, my father wiped his brow with one thick arm, reeking of steaks.

When the time arrived to assemble her, they took away my stool and made me stand behind them as my father cut open the moulds.

He took out two perfect dainty feet and put them on my stool.

Ilse clasped her hands. "Hephaestus!" she sighed.

Father melted the ankles with torch fire and fastened her legs on, then continued with all of her parts, until he'd built a perfect little girl, four feet tall. Her waist curved like a real girl's, with a subtle flash of rib and teeny breast mounds. She even had a belly button. Between her legs puckered dainty little lips. My father heated the patch above them with his torch and stuck on tiny black hairs plucked from a skink. With great excitement, Ilse unwrapped a brown paper package. Inside flashed a mound of beautiful, shiny black human hair. They arranged it strand by strand on her head, around the centre of a perfect part. With a pair of gold scissors, Ilse cut a fringe. She took a paintbrush and two glass jars from a pocket of her apron, and painted my sister's lips and her cheeks pink. Her eyes, Ilse painted a beautiful bright purple. Lifting her legs one at a time, they dressed her in a pair of cotton knickers with a bunched-up waistband.

My father took a scalpel and cut a deep block out of my sister's chest, scraping it smooth on all sides. With a plumbing snake, he dug out a tunnel from the top of the empty hole in her chest up to the back of her mouth. He bent over the cardboard box on the floor, flicking his fingers as if coaxing a rabbit out of a hat, and carefully lifted out the shiny object, a metal contraption. It was a naked music box with ratchets, a steel comb, a train wheel with pinions attached, and a winding click. He set this in the girl's chest, then took a long metal worm from the box, filtered it down the hole in her mouth, and screwed it into the mainspring. To the top of the worm at the back of her throat he screwed a large fly, about two inches long. He reached into her mouth and turned it. A deranged polka from Andrei Górecki's Symphony No. 4 rang out on her steel comb, which did not surprise me at all. My father liked to pair pretty and grotesque things. He was a natural contrarian.

Cupping my sister's cheek, Ilse waited for the music box to wind down to plump, disconnected notes. "Oh, Christiana. Hello, sweet Christiana."

When she heard her name, Christiana clicked her purple eyes up to look straight into Ilse's. Ilse squeaked, but I laughed. I knew Christiana had been watching and listening ever since she had a head.

My father smiled, gleaming with sweat and pride. They each took one of Christiana's hands and, bending at the same time, kissed her on the cheeks.

"Oh, those are nice kisses," Christiana said in a brassy voice. "I love you. And you," she said, stretching out her arms to me. "You are my sister, is that true? I love you the most. But who tied your arms like that?"

Ilse blushed. My father cleared his throat. "It is a case of the lesser of two evils..."

"They tied me up because I scared them."

"*You* scared them?" Christiana grinned. If she'd had real skin, her nose and eyes would have crinkled, but her features stayed flat and her cheeks didn't lift. "I'm not afraid of you," she laughed. "You're the only one here the same as me."

She looked past me at her new world, gaping at the reflection of the room and all its tools in the little girl's mirror hanging on the wall. I remembered when I first saw that mirror. I thought it was a doorway into the room of the room.

Then she saw mother bear's head floating in the tub.

"Who did that?" she screamed, crossing her arms over her music-box heart. "Where is the inside of her? Mother?"

The wax around Christiana's eyes sagged slightly, blearily melted. The jiff jumped in me. What had melted the wax around Christiana's eyes? Was there a heat that came from inside her?

"Mother." She buried her poisoned head into Ilse's chest and sobbed. "Mother, it wasn't you or Father who took her away from herself, was it?"

"It was me," I said.

Christiana lifted her head. She walked to me with jerky little steps, holding her hands out for balance. She put her smooth hands on my smooth shoulders and stared into my face, unbreathing.

I knew, as we touched, that we had doubled in size.

"Let them live, sister," she said.

She tottered past me out the door, into the world. Clouds gathered like wadding above the house, tittered over by little off-red birds. The ridge of pine stood reflected in the lake, as if someone had grabbed the treeline and cracked it open. Loose nets of blackflies waited to throw themselves on my father and Ilse. Mounds of ice in the deepest nooks of the forest wafted nourishing chills.

She bent at the waist and picked up a twig. With it, she reached inside her chest and plucked out a little song on her steel comb.

My father clapped and swivelled on the balls of his feet. I had never seen him move with such gallant smoothness, not even when he'd walked out of the chapel with Ilse. "How did I *do* that?" He hopped up and down, swinging his elbows like a tin soldier. "I just created a being with a musical sensibility. Ilse!"

"Hephaestus, when you made her, your soul must have been in a pure state of sweetness and generosity."

He squinted his eyes, frowning.

Ilse took Christiana by the elbow and led her toward the house. My new sister called over her shoulder, "Sister? Are you coming?"

So I was invited back in.

"Can I trust you not to burn us all in our beds?" my father said quietly before he unbound me.

"Of course. I am a very dignified person."

⋙ ⋘

That night at supper Christiana put bits of bread in her mouth and pretended to eat them, laughing hysterically. Afterwards, Ilse painted Christiana's toenails, while my father snuck down to my old bedroom with a screwdriver.

I poked my head in later and saw that my room had been transformed. Where there once was a hard plank between two sawhorses—my cot—there was now a bunkbed against the wall, with primrose quilts. Under the window sat a table with a vase of wildflowers on it, and some dusting cloths for our baths. On the floor was a hook rug of a pink-and-purple peacock. In the closet hung rows of dresses. White curtains blew around my father, who was bent over, plugging in a lamp. It was not one of his own lamps, which had stands made of three deer legs strapped together. This lampstand had a wooden tripod with two shelves. On the bottom shelf sat a piggy bank; on the top was a windup snow globe—containing a ceramic hippo and a monkey hugging each other—that played a lullaby. The lamp cast a warm glow.

He turned and saw me. His face was as honest as any cornered beast's.

"Go on," he coaxed. "Git. Go see your sister."

His voice was oddly gentle. His short, thick hands seemed relaxed. And he was barefoot. My father never showed his feet.

"Where are your socks?"

"My feet were hot."

"Father, does a man in good health have hot feet?"

I was starting to wonder about the effects of arsenic.

"Probably not."

"Maybe you are sick."

"In more ways than one. Buff Duck?"

"Yes."

"I'm glad the room's prettier for you now."

"Yes," I said.

<hr />

Christiana is affectionate. Even now, after she plays a song on her steel comb with a surgeon's needle, she will say, "Can I have a kiss for my performance?"

She has written dozens of songs. She still sings some of the originals—"Mother Gives Fox a Frozen Weiner," "Father Takes Down the Traps," "Brace the Wing and Let Them Live"—although after one of those, she will first stoke the fire through a protective leather glove before asking, in a voice that sounds a thousand years old, for her kiss.

They kissed her a hundred times a day. She sat on their laps and they kissed her. She always wanted to play airplane, so they grabbed her by the wrists and spun her around, then kissed her. She crawled into bed with them when she had a bad dream and they rolled over in their sleep and kissed her.

No wonder they got sick in just a few months.

One overcast day, we went to market as a family, with all our stock. Christiana and I wore floppy hats in case the sun came out, but otherwise I was more exposed than I'd ever been in public, wearing a dress. My black cloak hung back at home in the woods, in a place only I knew about.

"You look nice, Buff Duck," Father croaked, dabbing his neck with a towel.

"I am so thirsty," Ilse gasped in the truck, patting her thumping heart. She stared at the whitish lines that had recently appeared on her fingernails.

She had made a little sign out of broken pieces of driftwood that said *Liquidation Sale. Deal of the Century.* It had taken her ten tries. *Deal of the Centurion, Liquid Sale.*

"I don't know why I keep making mistakes," she'd said. "Where's my focus?"

We sold everything. All our rugs, lampstands, and stoles, our decorative birds on mounts and in glass globes on pieces of gold string, all our hats and muffs and fingerless gloves, all our coyote masks. To a local wildlife centre we gave a loon, a woodchuck, and also brother and sister bear, who we had stuffed and mounted on logs, very artfully, so they climbed with great earnestness toward heaven or hell, depending which way you held the log.

The shoppers still whispered about us.

Did he mail order another one?

He's got a whole harem.

Why doesn't anyone do anything about it—religious freedom?

But Christiana smiled at everyone and they smiled back. Ilse and my father sat on the back of the truck waving at people. My father's round face was dark red, and on our drive in, Ilse kept having to pee, each time barely making it out of the truck. Her urine looked like tea.

At night I heard my father and Ilse whispering about how to make a living in a way that did not upset Christiana. They sighed. "Oh well. We'll think of something tomorrow. Maybe we can grow some nuts."

As they sickened, Christiana hovered over them with her smooth, pretty face, adjusting the umbrellas over their hammocks and feeding them crab-apple juice from apples she had picked with her poisonous hands. I asked her how they liked their juice and their soup and suggested lots of recipes Christiana might make for them.

It's hard not to rush death, knowing it's coming. I don't like surprises and I don't like waiting. I liked watching my bears play, but after that experience, I feel safer stroking a mounted bird's back, and knowing that's how it'll always be.

⋙⋘

"Little Buff Duck," my father called hoarsely from his bed as I passed one day in the hall.

He lay on his stomach with one hand off the mattress. A colour I did not trust myself to detect stained his eyes. Yellow, perhaps. Over his shoulder, Ilse lay on her back with the blanket pulled up to her chin and her head rolled away.

I pointed at her. "Is that what I look like?"

My father's mouth was black, his fillings shone. He looked at me with that familiar combination of neediness and accusation.

"You told me once that I gave you a feeling. What was it?"

I knelt next to his face and put my nose close to his. Clusters of warts had sprung up around his tear ducts and the bottom of his face was red as a beet.

"You make me feel like I don't exist."

Water came from between his warts and rolled into a little wet patch on the mattress. "I'm sorry I hurt you. Little Buff Duck? Are you listening? Will you forgive me, please?"

"Only if you tell me I am real."

"You're real." He squeezed his eyes shut.

"I forgive you."

"I always knew you were real," he whispered. "It was myself I didn't trust was real."

"I already said I forgive you."

Sometimes he talks too much.

❧

I feel so happy. When I choose to be kind, I am very powerful. It is wonderful to have someone to care for.

I am very protective of my sister. I make sure she has a bath every day, wetting a tea towel with a lukewarm vinegar solution and wiping her down.

"Tell me about your nightmare," I say, wringing my towel.

"I am floating in the sea. I'll never melt, nothing will ever eat me, the shore is never in sight, I cannot play my music box, there are no boats. My best friend is a black balloon floating in the sky. It drifts far, far away until I can't see it anymore, but if I squint I can see it. But even when I can barely see it, I can't tell if it's there or not."

"Good thing we're far from the sea. Good thing a dream is just a dream."

"Sister?"

"Yes, Christiana?"

"Nothing wants to eat us. And we don't want to eat anything."

"This is true."

"How do we fit into the whole thing, then?"

"What thing?"

"All the creatures eat one another, don't they? They're all together eating each other."

"Except for bees," I say. "Bees drink the flowers and the flowers are still there."

"Do all the creatures get sick and die?"

"They do."

"Is that what happened to Father and Mother?"

"Yes."

"You do such a wonderful job of caring for me, sister. But do you think one day, when we go to town, we will find new parents who will adopt us and love us?"

"If that's what you want."

"And I will play them songs and kiss them, and our new parents won't get warts on their eyes and their hearts won't go bad on them?"

I get jealous when she dreams up new parents, and sometimes I almost tell her that her kisses are the kisses of death. But I want only sweetness for Christiana. When she asks for a story from a time before she was born, I tell her only the good ones, when he was kind to me and called me Little Buff Duck.

The secret of Christiana's deadliness is the only thing I've ever possessed.

I think about it all the time, but I can only talk about it with Father. I have mounted him very artfully by the foot, which rests on a log. He leans with his arm across his knee. His other arm hangs down, holding his axe as he squints into the distance between the trees, enjoying the aplomb of the woods. It is a lifelike pose—I saw him make it in the middle of many September afternoons while chopping wood. I believe he would be pleased with the fineness of my work, even though I couldn't do anything about the discoloration of his face.

Ilse I put in *Polynesia*, on a swing, so when Christiana is sad she can sit on her lap and I can push them and I don't have to think up comforting words, which are not my forte.

"Father?" I ask from my wet stone with wadding on my lap, carefully wiping blood off black plumage. "You will not tell Christiana I sometimes come here to my secret place to cool and mount the crows she doesn't know I catch?"

Everyone needs a little something for themselves.

"Father? Don't you think I finally look like myself?"

Yes. You are gleaming, dark, and debonair, and I believe everything about you.

He's right. I am extremely believable. My eyes are black as oil, my hands long, thin, and peaked with talons. I am very tall. Black wings spring out of my neck. They are undersized and in good humour, especially on bright days when they acquire a purple glint. I have a beak but I cannot fly, like an octopus.

When I look in the mirror and the crow looks back at me and says, "I love you, even though you make me nervous," the jiff inside goes thump, thump—just twice, but still.

"Father, I have another question. Does knowing something about Christiana that she doesn't know herself make me more real than she is?"

That one is rhetorical. I am more real than I've ever been.

FELIX BAUMGARTNER'S GUARDIAN ANGEL

I HATE YOUR AMBITION, FELIX.

I hate that on the blank line next to *Career*, you write *daredevil*. I hate that your father is a carpenter, which has led you to make personal comparisons between yourself and Christ. I hate that in an interview, you advocated *a moderate dictatorship led by experienced personalities coming from the private economy*.

But up we go, hey, Felix? Up to space we go, pulled by a balloon.

I wish I weren't your guardian angel.

There you are, waving goodbye to the cameras. You're thinking of the love you didn't make last night to your fiancée, Nicole Oetl, Miss Lower Austria 2006. You're imagining that the libidinal energy you didn't expend is now fusing at a spot in the centre of your pelvis. You envision it flaring across your chest and firming into armour. You feel that, by not making love to Nicole but instead hovering your hands over her womb while gazing existentially into her eyes, you have made her want your return so badly—now her want is another force in your arsenal of stocked forces.

Now you're sitting in the capsule. The door is shut. Your knees are at your chest.

Do you think it's comfortable squeezing behind you in a floating capsule, Felix?

Well, it is. Surprisingly comfortable. You always smell a little of fresh pepper.

You take your sweet time responding to Joe Kittinger, Capsule Communicator. Joe is an eighty-four-year-old ex-prisoner of a North Vietnamese war camp. The two of you are competitive because Joe holds the world record for this jump. In 1960, he leapt from 107,800 feet and accelerated through a free fall that lasted four minutes and thirty-six seconds. Joe wants only the best for you. But you'll make him wait. You imagine you can transmogrify into an indestructible god-substance if you direct all of humanity's energy toward yourself.

Hear me, Felix. I bring you tidings of counterforces.

Some people want you to die today.

Your mother, Eva, does not consciously will you to die. But if your parachute fails, and you speed into a human meteor that disappears into a shallow pit of iron and dew, then the pain she suffers right now on your behalf—not to mention her pride at being watched by millions of people, which makes her feel insincere—would end, and she could go home to Austria with the glorious tale of your tragic descent.

"Everything is in the green. Doing great," says Joe Kittinger.

We are 60,229 feet above earth. It is minute 59:59 of your ascent.

I have projected an astral stream that mimics the condensation of your breath through the opaque surface of your pressurized mask. Why did I do it? I want Joe Kittinger to cancel the operation. Do not turn your back on earth, Felix.

You radio Joe to tell him everything is not in the green; your visor is fogging up when you breathe. Everyone worries that your helmet is cracked. If it is, the blood will boil in your head as soon as you exit the capsule.

Still, off-camera, you tell Joe: "Let's continue. God is on my side."

Felix, you just broke the record for highest manned balloon flight at 114,038 feet. Good for you. Now the balloon is higher than your original target and we're still climbing at a thousand feet per second.

Joe Kittinger is running through your checklist. He says, "I need you to respond to my commands. From now on it gets really serious, Felix."

You don't respond because I have wrapped my ethereal body around your head and beg you telepathically, *Don't open the door*. Ah, that pepper scent. It comes from inside you.

The door opens. You press the button that moves your seat forward. Now your legs hang outside the capsule on the jumping platform. You stand.

Joe Kittinger says, "Felix, jump. Felix, you have to jump."

Felix, are we up here looking down—or down there, in an Arctic region, gazing up at solar storms? What if the black of space is a curtain protecting us from the blazing face of God, and the stars are holes in the curtain? But no, all of this is God. These green-and-blue cosmic anomalies of earth spinning backwards over her axis. The universe is a cyclops and this is its eye. I'm sorry you can't see this because I fogged up your mask.

"Into my father's arms," you yell.

I am with you, Felix. I will rock you in waves until you come out of your spin.

Do you hear that, Felix? Your heart makes a noise in space one thousand metres behind us.

Felix, right now you have no features or family or mean politics or pride.

Felix, everything alive is taking a turn in heaven. To be awake!

You beautiful spark, you spinning shard of star.

Felix, I love you.

WHAT BOTHERS A WOMAN OF THE WORLD

FIRST OF ALL, the name of the creature who follows me around: Agvagvat. I watch my mouth in the mirror call her, *Hey, Agvagvat*, and I can't stand it. Agvagvat isn't an attractive word to say. When I make those guppy sounds, I look very middle-aged.

This evening, she followed me down the frozen food aisle of the Safeway, using her flat body to propel herself forward in the manner of a sea slug. Agvagvat is squishy, jelly-like but harder to tear. She is purply-pink, with frills along her back that look delicate and sedate, as if they would sway in water, but in fact they are firm and entirely under Agvagvat's control. A few terrible, thin hairs coil here and there. Watching her manoeuvre her boneless back across a mangled perogy, you might think she has picked up the hairs on her journey. She hasn't. Even though she travels in direct contact with the ground, she is surprisingly clean, or, at least, nothing sticks to her.

Agvagvat is a good friend. She doesn't understand hard facts very well—you could never ask her to give a financial presentation, for example—but when it comes to emotional subtlety, in my opinion there is no one as...well, if perceptive isn't exactly the right word, let's say: there is no one as *accommodating* as Agvagvat.

This morning, in the UberX en route to my presentation, where I was to deliver management's decision to terminate the Fund, I was very supercilious to my driver, Moe. Not smug, not condescending or clipped—but you could tell I basked in my own magnanimity.

Traffic on the Gardiner was gridlocked. "Take Lakeshore," I said.

I was feeling proud of myself. I was thinking, *Here we go, Woman of the World, things to do, people to speak to*. But as we travelled past the ostentatious gates of Exhibition Place—its aura of Victorian enchantment that, after all these years, still wants to impress Daddy but hasn't figured out how to—a wave of despair rushed over me. A wave of self-loathing, actually.

Look at the rush I am in, how eager I am to please authority. In my ambition, I strive to be the authority, but I know if I succeed, the whole fiction of authority would crumble because, let's face it: I know myself. I know the many ways in which I am not knowledgeable, courageous, or serene.

Worse, if I'm already addicted to the rush—to the relief!—of there being a point to my adult life, after all, given a little power and applause, what *wouldn't* I do, what dark instruction wouldn't I obey, from an even greater authority—so comforting—who flatteringly assures me that I've been specially chosen to complete a heinous task?

I'm no hero. That's what I realized.

Seeing me disturbed by existential troubles, it was Agvagvat who dragged herself onto my lap and sat quietly under my hands, offering me the encouragement that sometimes only weight and mass can give. In return, I poured some of my coffee into the hole along her back, deep into the ridge I think functions as a toothless mouth, though it doesn't seem to chew, or to swallow; it merely smacks open and closed, as if responding to air in a way that isn't quite like breathing either. The coffee went in and dribbled out, gummed by the slow squelching of her hole.

"Ouch," she said. "Hot."

"Can I touch her?" Moe asked sweetly.

He'd been watching her the whole time, of course.

"What? Here in the car?"

"Why not?"

"Well, not if you ask first."

Moe smirked—he knew he'd got me. "You're so funny. You let me touch Agvagvat all the time, but the moment I say her name out loud you die of shame."

Such a Moe thing to say. He isn't only my Uber driver, you see. But the stakes of our affair are so low, when I'm next to him it's as if this all took place a few years ago and I'm reliving it in memory. The moment he pays me any attention, I pay my attention to Agvagvat.

I'm quiet about it, but I like to secretly tickle her so she wakes up, then I press on the right places until she's as happy as a cat being scratched, though she is far less obvious about her enjoyment. The only sign of Agvagvat's enjoyment is a very slight reaching toward, as though she is shifting in her sleep. Because her pleasure looks so small, I suspect Agvagvat of thriving on minutiae, although she tells me the experience of being scratched is "like a high wave." It doesn't seem like Agvagvat is lying; certainly she wouldn't gain anything by it, except for more scratches, I suppose. Still. The way she says she feels is so different from the way she looks...

She annoys me so much I have to tuck her under the waist of my pants, even if it pinches her, in my best attempt to pretend she isn't there. "Forget it for the next few hours," I tell her. "Go to sleep."

Actually, she isn't annoying at all. She's kind and restrained, not showy. She isn't upset when I ignore her.

This evening, at Safeway, I pushed the cart toward the frozen lasagna at a speed I knew she would not be able to match, given her limbless body. But she did not whine, *Hey, can we walk together, please?* She gave me my space.

Agvagvat stopped to look through one of the freezer doors at a box of edamame. And even though she did nothing wrong in slowing to look, even though every single shopper in the frozen food aisle also stopped to look at vegetable potstickers or bags of blueberries or whatever, I nonetheless saw the people behind Agvagvat grit their teeth. They veered their carts around her, maybe gave her a little *we're-all-in-this-together* grin if she happened to turn around, but I knew—I saw it in their eyes and in the closeness of their carts to Agvagvat's body—that they had a powerful urge to run over Agvagvat, even to jump up and down on Agvagvat.

Feeling protective, I went back and said, in a voice loud enough for all to hear, "Everyone's in a rush, eh?"

And she said, in her murmuring, underwater voice with its eternal mission to coax me toward a moral life, "You've done worse things today than buy a frozen lasagna. Just feed it to the kids and make something from scratch on the weekend. Do that and I'll let you pour more coffee down my hole. I know you like to look inside."

Then we had to look at one another companionably and pretend nobody wanted to run her over in the first place! It was oppressive.

But worse, far worse, is when I'm back home with Denis and the kids. As I'm doing something banal and vindictive—say, unwrapping a frozen lasagna and plotting in a secret chamber of my heart to fill up on salad and let everyone else eat the chemicals—there is a guilty silence from the next room.

I go stand in the doorway and see my two daughters, side by side. They are staring down at Agvagvat, who sits on our moss-green ottoman looking up at them. It seems they went through the kitchen drawer while I was in the bathroom, even though they're only two and four! One of them has a metal kebab stick, the other a meat thermometer. They are watching the puckering little puncture wounds they made in Agvagvat dribble inoffensive ooze that's clear as spit. They bend to see if there's an odour.

As the wounds begin their quick, thorough process of self-healing, and my kids stare, astonished, traumatized for having been the ones to inflict mutilation, I find that I understand them completely. I, too, look down at Agvagvat sometimes and have an urge to dig my fingers into her squishiness, to tear her open. Buried in that urge is a hope, or a fear, that if I tear her open I will discover there is no end to her, she's deeper than anyone realized—that if I stick my hand far down into Agvagvat's irritating softness, I will light upon the hardness buried inside her like a tooth, the powerful core of Agvagvat.

Of course, Agvagvat contains no key, no mysterious core. She's in pain, that's all. It's unjust. She stares back up at my kids, the ones who hurt her, and that is when I see it: Agvagvat's hope. Hope for what? For a day when she will sit alongside a real friend and they will enjoy a simple pleasure in common. And this, really, is why she terrifies me.

What right has a creature as exposed as Agvagvat to bear such hope?

PASTORAL

ACORNS

THE SHEPHERD HIKES THROUGH TANGLED BRAKE to his secret place, followed by his ewes. This daily trek is the only hardship he demands of them. He knows they are afraid of the forest's confinement, of the things that fall from trees. Their pupils are enormous. They are not made to seek in shadow; they avoid sharp contrasts between light and dark, which instantly vault them into despair.

It is here at Little Ox Oak, on the bank of the Moira River by the ruins of Honeywell Shrine, that he brought the dairymaid the first time she begged him to make love to her. When he couldn't enter her, not then or since, because he was too soft, she lay on top of him, kissed the tight folds of skin under his eyes, his small, strong nose, the red taint of his cheeks, and called him beautiful.

Through no coincidence, this place is also where the shepherd performs his ritual. He moves slowly, but never stops, because in the woods his sheep must always go forward. That is how they know they will eventually leave. First, he picks up all the acorns that have fallen since yesterday. If the acorns are perfect, without holes or cracks, stems as pert as they would be in a picture of an acorn, he hurls them into the river. The broken acorns, the ones with their brittle mushroom caps severed from their gleaming bodies, he puts in his mouth and swallows.

These nuts subdue the angry dog inside of him, the dog that growls *My girl's another's*.

It is the ritual itself, correctly performed, that prevents the dairymaid from leaving him. His dairymaid, who churns cream back in the village with a blind, childlike seriousness that shocks him with joy each time he thinks of it.

But he must hurry. Not just because tonight is the harvest moon junket, the night they live for, but because out on the wide emerald field banded in sky, just paces from the darkness of the woods, he had left a lamb tied by a rope to a boulder. The wolves are shy and prefer the night. But if he lingers, they will come for the lamb, baaing alone too temptingly. Right now, he knows, the wolves are creeping inch-by-inch through the toppled vines and rich mosses.

This is the dangerous part of the shepherd's ritual. Though each broken acorn must be swallowed before wolves reach the lamb, he will walk at the same slow pace, bending, skimming the grass with his hand. The ritual is torturous at the best of times, but since the monk came, since the dairymaid began her lessons at the monastery, it has become unbearable.

More broken acorns than ever before pebble his secret place, as though each night a beast with hard feet walks there.

SCHOLARSHIP

The monk climbs the cool tower stairs of the Monastery of Rahab the Red Cord. He sits at his desk and gazes out a stone window. The country air is sweet and thick. He inhales the taste of hay. Delicious.

Far down to his right lies the village, green and gold in the afternoon light, with its brown cabins at once weathered and kempt. One feels as if in the presence of a favourite grandmother. Crows caw from the steadings, sheep wander the hills, donkeys bray at horses that sulkily nip one another. Straight ahead is the most famous forest in all the land, a booming explosion of fat, fluttering green. He stares at the ruin peeking through the trees. It was a native temple, he's been told, the shrine of a forgotten bird goddess. Once forgotten, twice dead.

He caws out the window, hoping a monk on another floor of the tower will lift his head and scan the eaves for a graveyard bird.

If he finishes this translation by tomorrow, he will go exploring in the woods again and lose himself all morning in the crumbled sanctum's mystery. The monk loves the dead temple priestesses and wants to learn their rites. What an absurd, crucial job, to fasten this frail world to the Divine so the earth does not spin off alone into the abyss.

Not yet.

He moves his ink, the old book, the box containing pages of translation, to the edges of his desk. From his robe he takes a round of pressed cottage cheese. The dairymaid gave it to him when he stopped to say hello, wrapping it in a piece of her apron she tore apart right in front of him, claiming it was old. Cupping her cheese in both hands as though it is a tender head, he gently peels back the apron. The monk bends over the cheese and imbibes its odour of musk. He nuzzles his nose into the soft, warm flesh of it, grazes the white mound with his lips. Mouthful after mouthful, he devours the cheese. He licks film off the fabric.

Finally, he opens his eyes.

97

Well, he has a problem with ecstasy and the descent from ecstasy. Remember his brothers-in-law carrying him down the parade in a hammock to the Rahabians, nearly starved and mortified in flesh, three twists a day of the screw through his navel, the Father, the Son, and Holy Ghost? What trite on-the-nose bullshit. He holds a shaking hand to his face. His sisters' husbands had rolled their eyes as they used him to exercise their limp compassion. Odious little tubers. He's glad he trained their goodness by making them take care of him.

Sighing, he folds the soiled piece of apron into a square and puts it into the pocket of his robe. He brushes remnants of curd onto the windowsill for the birds and taps his papers back to the centre of his desk.

WORKING

Heels deep, thighs strained, palms burning, belly tense as a flexed tongue. The dairymaid churns cream in the middle of Plainfield's village green.

Her attention is split between choosing which unique ingredients must go in next to flavour her butter in a way the monk will find surprising and rare, and revelling in the admiration of men. Old men rinsing dye from wool, young men carrying planks of wood to the stables and stopping to rest on the fence, men missing an eye or an ear who sit on stumps plucking feathers out of geese their wives have killed. Boys skipping down the lane with their fathers' lunches, crusts of bread and pressed cottage cheese as sectile as raw goose flesh, wrapped in cloth.

She remembers the monk's quiet intensity when she'd sat across from him at the library table yesterday and read from the Psalms, *You distanced my friends from me, you made me disgusting to them.* Did he know that line forced her to say the truth? "Did you choose this one because it's the story of your life?" she'd desperately quipped. He blushed.

He is so young—four months younger than her! She lifts her arms high, to flaunt the blue cotton bodice dark under her breasts. Her frilled white sleeves stick to her. Fastened to a string around her neck is the stone her own shepherd gave her, which he had chipped from the peak of Mount Mary. She imagines him bracing his sweet, round face against the wind, scanning dark volcanic crags brushed in snow until he sees this piece, the one that glints. Her heart leaps; she shoves the stone into her mouth.

From a little pouch at her waist she takes lemon rind and a square of leather, and drops them into the thickening cream. She plunges faster, picturing the cellar of the cruck house where she and the shepherd live, and, on a dark, clean shelf, the butter chilling in the jewellery box she has kept from her old life.

Soon—as soon as she perfects this recipe—(any day now, she hopes!) she will wind the box's gold key, and a white bear will pirouette over the yellow tundra of bitter and sweet, strange and subtle, wild, careful butter. The monk will taste it, he will be amazed, he will introduce her butter to those who understand and love such things, and they will invite her into their world. She will be home.

PROMISES

As the monk watches the idyll of labour below him, the milking and planting and shearing and drying of darnel, he has the feeling that life in the country, for all its naturalness, lacks the liberty of civilization.

Six months ago, during a cruel, black January, he came to Rahab from the city of Boolavogue. He finds that, unlike the bureaucrats and fashion hounds there, the labourers here perform work he believes to be as sacrosanct, as necessary, and—in a way that pleases him—as degraded as his own. Still, no trinkets for sale at booths, no fawny red-boots crossing their legs on sunny patios over powdery lunches, no tossing simples in the fountain at the centre of the square, no booksellers, no theatre, no strolling over a bridge lost in existential chit-chat with his friend and most beloved father figure, the Mennonite Reverend Dyck. There is nothing impractical, no act disconnected from its clearly defined result. The only excess here is beauty.

All of this is why he came to the country in the first place. Still, he is surprised, now, to miss the freedom of a manicured garden, the autonomy to shape nature for his useless pleasure.

He looks down at the picture he has just made on his parchment, of the sylvan view from this window. He has made no additions, taken no leaps of fancy. There are the fields, the woods, the village, the domed roof of the temple pushing through the trees, all of it framed by the stone window, just as he sees it. On the winding path he draws his grandfather pointing a rifle at the back of a girl in a blue dress.

From the wood, a wolf howls. *Exactly*, he thinks, scanning the trees with pleasure.

Remember what the brothers had said as he lay in the ward recovering? "Christ does not need to be such a cruel wife. At her very worst, she may be a bit dull for a man your age. Be more practical. Between now and Salvation, there is a life."

He throws down his quill, sinks his face in his hands, and shudders. He should not have done it, he should not have told the dairymaid that he knew people in Boolavogue who may be interested in distributing her butter. The only person he knows remotely connected to the culinary world is the chef at the college where he took his theology degree, a friendly but depressed Jordanian who fed them simple roasts and soups because he hated the decadent sauces at the centre of Boolavoguian cuisine. What would Blady do with a sample of artisanal butter?

The monk made this promise to the dairymaid because he wished he could help her, and forgot, way out here, that wishing for something does not make it true. Also—this thought makes him press his head into his desk—he wanted to have something of hers, a thing that would make it impossible for her not to keep coming to him. He wanted her hope.

And yet he admires the manipulative efforts of his blind desire. It feels both like a part of him and like something else. His desire turns him and everyone he cares about into an instrument to attain its end. He loves his desire, he has faith in it.

RUINS

The dairymaid goes to the monastery for lessons, but the shepherd takes no holiday from his ewes or his ritual. In the rich tangle of his secret place, among stones cascading from the abandoned temple as though the temple wears a skirt of ruin, every acorn knocked to the ground is broken. The shepherd keeps his pace, bends, skims the grass with his hand, finds a broken acorn, swallows it. The ache in his gut means she will not leave him.

His ewes huddle around his legs. If one of them raises her head to bleat, he growls.

The shepherd swallows another broken acorn. He is tempted to pretend he doesn't see the acorns in the grass and to step on them, to grind them into the dirt until they disappear. But he does not give in to this temptation. Acorn after acorn he puts in his mouth and swallows.

Now the shepherd breaks his pace, faster and faster, until he is constantly bent with his hand in the grass, a three-legged half of an insect. He cannot help it. A high, long yelp is buried in his throat, and now it screams along the roof of his mouth.

Finally, his hand lights upon clear ground. Muttering thanks, his heart pounding, the shepherd stands up. His feet press firmly into the ground as he stares out at the river.

SALT

The dairymaid's shoulders burn with a glorious power as she plunges again and again into her barrel. The smell of beaten cream is sweet, with an undercurrent of womb. It will be so light and delicious when chilled. But warm milk makes the dairymaid sick unless she gives herself over to it entirely, glories in the hot squelch, the still golden air, the brown tendrils curled around her throat, her clenched bowels, her saltiness. Her body produces miraculous fluids, with which she would paint the countryside if it weren't already so green and yellow.

Far off, out of a copse of tall, swaying maple, an exaltation of larks! Nature loves her. She imagines charming snakes from sand and commanding spiders to swarm her enemies. Only she knows their horrible ecstasy, because she comes to all the loathed things with joy, as a playmate.

Against her will, she seeks them out. Beyond the ring of parched men, the other dairymaids hang corn swag on the barn door, drape tables in paisley, decorate platters with apricots, stir rye into punch bowls with ladles a foot long, designed by their grandmothers for this purpose. Others lace together on the miller's porch, and twist each other's long hair. The dairymaid stares at the pink and periwinkle ribbons fluttering in a basket, so the women won't think she's staring at them. The ribbons will be braided into all the hair so everybody knows the heads match.

She is the only one not invited.

The dairymaid sucks on her shepherd's stone for comfort and tries to determine the amount of salt that would show off her butter's sweetness. Out of the corner of her eye, she feels the young men watching her with a candour she now realizes is violent. They are lined up, all four of them, with their elbows on the fence, tearing blades of grass and talking, she hopes, about their flocks. She no longer feels like frolicking in their desire and suspects they are making her their game.

She stops churning and rubs her chafed palms together. Although she invited the monk to the harvest moon junket, she dreads the moment he will see how alone and friendless she is. It has been such a relief to spend time with someone who does not know her story. Tonight, all of that will be over.

HER STORY

Though everyone in Plainfield knows the broad sketches of her story, the dairymaid has often marvelled that no one really knows it. The result is exile: they think they know her, but do not understand any of the details, any of the densities.

They look at her and dream only of tantalizing horrors inflicted by the lord. She sees their wide eyes, their watering mouths. Oh, and don't they know the lord paid her richly for her ten years. They know it and they hate her for it. They call her vain, a gloater, Duchess Slut—or they used to call her these things, until the shepherd took up with her.

As the dairymaid rests against her pole and wipes her forehead with a rag, she thinks of herself eight years ago, in candlelight, at a stone table draped in white. The table held a spread of rare meats, olives from far, far away, fruits that tasted like clouds and sucked all the moisture from her mouth.

That old grotto was one of the only restaurants in Boolavogue where the country lord could still take his girl-wife, for the custom is repugnant to many. And yet he has had a girl-wife every decade since he was seventeen. It is simply the shape of a life that is as subject to fate and tradition as hers, and—he remarked frequently—hadn't he been gentle with her, even though no one stood at his shoulder ready to punish his unkindness, or to offer her recourse to any law? He did not even feel tempted to be cruel, not anymore, not even when they misbehave, as children will, even the most intelligent and beautiful children.

She had sat there with painted blue eyelids, in silence, not eating. She'd known this time was coming—she knew of her liberation right from the beginning, had been told on numerous occasions, "This time we have is very special, it will not last. Soon enough you will be free of me forever, so let's not fight. Do not sulk or scream, tantrums are for ordinary girls and you, my pet, well, I chose you because you are an angel."

She remembers the lord's eyes, blue fertilizations floating across a cooked egg. He reached over and moved her full plate to one side. Then, from a ledge built right into the stone walls of the place, he took a large wooden box, the object she had refused to acknowledge. The lord placed the box before him—this only gave him pleasure of the saddest kind, he told her—and pushed it across the table.

She lifted the lid.

The brightness of the seven tear-shaped diamonds, dangling from a neck band, was so shocking she gasped. Not because she had a particular love of gems, but how could she not be consoled by such excess, excited by the outrageous freedom it gave her? It was a magic necklace that turned her from a peasant into a queen. Now people would flock to her—she could love, patronize, be seen and admired and envied, instead of locked up in a castle. Seven diamonds for his girl-wife on her seventeenth birthday, in the year he turned fifty-seven. This was her payment for ten years of companionship.

But as soon as she felt all this relief, her stomach bent with revulsion. She had been taken by the lord against her will, her situation determined by fatalistic forces so large she could clearly distinguish herself from them, and so a part of her had gone untouched, her desire had gone untouched. Even as she had enjoyed aspects of her castle life— the satin chemises and truffle sauces, the deep baths in hot sheep's milk, the high view from her bedroom window of the lord's desolate hill, even the darkness of his empty halls and the unkempt, brittle gardens of his courtyards, so different from the lushness of the village below—she had always thought her life's desire was to escape the lord. But if she let this necklace gain her entrance to a glittering new life, wasn't she choosing not to escape him and the world he offered?

"Will you miss me?" she'd said, despite herself.

The lord had smiled. "Forget me. You're rich. Anything you want for the rest of your life, you can have."

"I want to go home," she'd said. "I want to go home to the castle."

RELIEF

Out of the woods now, across hills and pastures, the shepherd follows his ewes back to the village. They leap in their awkward penumbras; the lamb he saved darts between his legs, butts playfully into his thighs.

This is yet another secret, this is why he is the best of shepherds, a shepherd by heart as well as circumstance: he does not do it to lead. Paddock, field, hill, meadow—his ewes go where they like and he follows. Save for that hour a day in the woods, it's almost as though they have hired him to guard their meek, unadventurous journeys. The ewes even flirt with him. They spritz briny scents. He loves his little mistresses.

GIFTS

On the steep path between the Monastery of Rahab the Red Cord and the village of Plainfield, the monk watches an ox through a fence.

The ox lifts its head and bats its womanly eyes. A bloody rag wraps one of its hoofs. These people are pragmatists, as they must be, listening as they do all day and night to the guns and cannons of the perpetual war across a distant escarpment. If the ox is lame, they will cut its throat.

The monk has nothing, no apples, no honeycomb—again, he's forgotten those alms. He means to show kindness to beasts of burden, so he reaches over the low, wooden fence and tears up a handful of tall grasses. The creature shunts its way over, obediently, in pain, and in one heavy swing eclipses the monk's hand with its snout the size of a baby's bottom. This grass is hardly a gift, in fact the ox is going out of its way to accept something it already had but didn't want, and the sad gratefulness gathers like a walnut in the monk's throat. Here is God's charity unfolding out of the soul of this ugliest of bovines, for isn't it an act of charity to pretend the monk is gracious and this grass is a benefaction? Isn't it charity to hand over dominion to the monk and to bend one's clotted beard to the ground, so that the naked ape before you can call itself a man?

There is a noise behind him on the path. The soft chortling of sheep. Here they come around the bend, and there in the middle of the flock is the dairymaid's enormous, blue-eyed man. He tosses a thick oak staff with one hand. Clutched in the other is a bouquet of purple wildflowers.

The monk forces himself to look up, to be friendly but not as intimate as he feels. The shepherd's blue eyes are domes bursting with gold. They are eyes transcendent in their banality, like the sun in the sky, though his hair is grey and his face looks to have been stretched out and dried in a salt wind. The monk wants to chuckle, to show his carefree nature. Instead he holds up his finger and skewers the air. "You've caught me having a mystical experience with an ox."

The shepherd whistles. As they walk, the shepherd slightly ahead and the ewes jealously squeezing the monk out of the way, the monk thinks, We all suffer. At least this man has friends. Surely he is more in the world than I am.

The shepherd stops. He turns around.

One of his eyes is different, thinks the monk. One of his eyes doesn't blink. The monk stares into the shepherd's unblinking eye.

"She lives in a fantasy world," the shepherd says. "You can almost see it when you look at her, like a wreath of green-and-pink clouds. Dangerous weather that makes you remember your life."

The shadow of the shepherd's hand in the grass swoops with its claws out. He grips the monk's shoulder.

"Tornado weather, I'm telling you."

BEGGING

The dairymaid plunges again, again, again into her bucket. She rocks on her heels, palms so hot they feel like they might ignite. With each thrust the cream thickens. This kind of work only gets harder.

Now the old men sitting in a row drop scarlet nests of wet wool onto skins. They send her friendly winks, as if she has a secret only they know about. Through her sweaty grimace she winks back, but she knows this is false. She is not as in-tentionally coy as they give her credit for.

When the dye starts to burn, the grandfathers dip their arms in buckets of water. They rest their purple hands on their aprons to dry.

Something leaps like a grasshopper into her lips and she stumbles and swats it away. The old men cackle. She looks down. Beside her bucket, abject in their redness, lie a pair of fresh goose testicles half-covered in dust.

A noseless man on a stump leans over the dead bird in his lap and honks at her. She drops her pole, upends her bucket. The dairymaid grabs him by the shirt and yanks him off his stump. He shuts his eyes and honks. His pink oyster tongue quivers. All she wants to do is pinch it and tear. She squeezes his throat. The man might have laughed himself to death surrounded by his laughing friends, but—a miracle—the other dairymaids have rushed off the porch.

They drag her up to their spot and tie her arms to a chair with ribbons. "Why do you stay here just to act out?" they grumble. "You're rich. You could go to New York or To-ronto. If we were you, we'd have left years ago. Don't get us wrong—we don't blame you for what happened. Just, you know, for not leaving after. Be considerate. We're already too bound to the world by our children and our work, by our mothers, time, our men, and our bodies. We don't want more bonds like having to feel bad for you."

"My bad luck belongs to all of us," the dairymaid snarls. "Any one of you could have been in my shoes."

They sigh, shove a cup of frothy wine to her mouth, and tilt her chair back so she is forced to swallow.

"Then in fairness, your good luck belongs to us, too. Give us a diamond, why don't you."

RAIN

Damn the monk, with his thin neck and bugged eyes, silent but impossible to ignore, like a screaming head under water. The monk walks three awkward paces behind the shepherd, upsetting his ewes, who shuttle along without pausing to sniff or to bleat. And if you try to speak to him like a man, just watch him stop dead in the middle of the lane, scurry to gather himself, to remember his lines, this alien in a man's skin, face riveted on the progress of your soul. The shepherd hates anyone who can't banter.

We're all just trying to get by, he thinks. Why does this idiot have to blow the roof off our little world with his seriousness? Does he think we don't know we're going to die?

The shepherd wishes for an abandoned well, imagines the monk silently tripping, floating down, down in his robes, hitting his head on a stone.

There is a cosmic growl. The wind picks up. The storm he knew was coming has arrived. Now, as he walks through the gate into the green, the shepherd feels triumphant, as though he has brought this storm into the village to express his dismay. Let the monk prate, let the dairymaid console herself with bullshit from Rahab. He alone has nature's sympathy.

The sky's water breaks on his head. This storm, his sheep, the flowers he carries, even the bending trees roaring back at the wind: it is all a parade of the world's love for him.

Then he sees her.

Not alone, as usual, in the company of her green-and-pink clouds, but on the miller's porch, surrounded by other dairymaids, who laugh with the brutality of those who dream only of fabric and horses. As they tip a cup to her mouth and pull her chair back so she is forced to swallow, he feels a sudden, small pride in her for possibly winning friends.

But then, surges of grief.

APHRODITE

As the monk follows the shepherd into Plainfield, the sky is overcome with black, and rain cracks down. In front of him the shepherd does not change the pace of his long strides, but the monk leaps onto his toes, stumbles into an ewe, flings his arms up, and catches himself on the shepherd's shoulders.

The monk giggles, and is immediately mortified. Then he is ashamed for succumbing to the vanity that produces mortification. But he is also ashamed for the shepherd, who is giving himself up to the downpour by walking so slowly, with such determined, sacrificial manliness.

In a surge of rebellion, the monk darts around the shepherd and follows the villagers up some steps onto a white-roofed porch where, he is delighted to see, the women have already gathered.

"Welcome, Brother."

"Look, even our Brother is here!"

He is greeted by a dozen folk, patted on the back, handed a cup of mead. He then turns to watch, with contrition in his heart, as the shepherd finally mounts the stairs, unblinking and drenched to the bone. Only then does he see her.

She sits in the middle of everyone, tiny, lapping away at a cup stuffed into her dress. Her face is flushed, her eyes full with the strange combination of elation and sorrow he's seen on the face of new monks. Those are pink and purple hair ribbons tying her to the chair, but her hands are relaxed and she seems in no rush to be free.

Thunder rolls. Everyone yelps with delight. The shepherd cuts through the crowd, places his wet bouquet on her lap, and begins to untie the ribbons.

"Does everybody hate me?" she asks.

"Everybody loves you."

This is, the monk realizes, their usual exchange, and he flushes with awe at how well this other man knows her, when she is all the monk can think about, she fills every minute of his life.

But now everyone wants to speak with him. His cup is refilled. The dairymaid's explosion, and the presence of a holy man with a drink in his hand, have conspired with this hot summer storm to create a sense of mortal awareness that makes the harvest party feel urgent. For the first time since arriving at the monastery, the monk feels famous. It is a dangerous, prideful feeling, which he keeps in check by remaining quiet, speaking when spoken to or asking questions about their work. What market forces determine the price of wool? Is the almanac ever manipulated to sway certain kinds of production; for example, does it benefit anyone to say this will be a good year for cherries? These conspiracies are rapturous.

He watches her across his conversations and wills her to turn around, to witness his success at the party. Her beauty, he thinks, is as sharp and pink as a shell. He pictures a salty mollusc, a wound, a pearl. He imagines stepping on a piece of shell and cutting his foot, tearing out the clammy tongue and putting it in his mouth.

Miles away, the sky clears to reveal a patch of blue late afternoon.

"Look," the dairymaid says. "It's a portal that will take you into another day."

Suddenly she floats forward across the porch, as if riding the sea in the shell of the monk's imagining. Fire shoots up the monk's legs and he nearly drops his drink.

But no, she is not floating at all. She is in a rocking chair. Nor is his drink nearly dropped. It is clenched firmly in his fist and arriving, now, at his lips. He has just made a joke and everyone is laughing.

She turns, sees him, and jumps out of her chair. He raises his cup and nods at her, but she just marches off the porch and walks stiffly toward a row of prefabricated little sheds the monk realizes are homes, leaving him with his cup in the air, his little finger, for some reason, sticking straight out.

A cup knocks into his. "Cheers," the shepherd says.

TOYS

What is humiliation? is a question recently employed by the dairymaid.

Yesterday, she asked the monk. He brushed phantom crumbs off the library table into his hand and answered gently, for which she was grateful, "Humiliation is thwarted vanity— when the grandiose self-ideal is exposed as empty desire."

She had drawn her leg to her chest and hugged it. "But isn't there a more fundamental kind of humiliation that doesn't come from vanity? A kind that disturbs the basic idea of what it is to be human?"

"Basic idea like what?"

"Dignity, integrity, freedom."

He'd shrugged. "Who's to say those ideas aren't vanities?"

"What does one do," she'd said.

"If you live in a pooh."

"If you've been so humiliated you can't be a human anymore?"

"Become a monk."

The dairymaid thinks this conversation over. She sits straight as a queen on a long table, wearing her heavy diamonds, staring across the barn at the monk talking to the miller and his wife. He has not moved his feet an inch in half an hour, he is avoiding her. She pours another cup of mead down her throat, and it spills across her cheeks.

She remembers the time the monk told her all about his exploits, to defend himself against her teasing remarks about his chastity. How once, he'd been with every actress in a play he'd starred in. Once with Reverend Dyck's daughter, until he confessed to it and the three of them had a soul-baring talk into the night. And then Rachel Parsley: high society, anthropologist. How, after a term of flirtation at university high top dinners, he'd convinced her to break off her engagement to a financier. And how, despite his eventual forsaking of her, he still thought it was better she hadn't gone with one of those other kinds of people—the ones who measure the value of human life in terms of its potential contribution to output. How he'd saved her from the enemy.

Listening to him then, as he sat hunched over the table in the library at the Monastery of Rahab, talking about his affairs, the dairymaid had understood that the monk loved tortured, delectable dramas. She sat back, smiled, and accused him of needing an audience in order to love. She said unless someone was watching him—playgoers, concerned parents, anthropologists, God—he doubted his existence.

That he was a parasite seeking evidence of his existence from the pain he caused others.

She had been very proud of this speech.

A hand shatters the necklace's force field and grabs the dairymaid's arm. She looks up into the shepherd's unblinking eye, which looks like it is only pretending to be serious, and at the pink circles high on his cheeks. He wants her to see what it is like to be on the outside of him.

When everyone looked at her askance, he was the only one who brought her flowers—asphodel, bird of paradise, nearly impossible to find. But flowers are little lusts.

Over the glare of her diamonds she watches his eyes turn from impasses to wet impasses, then he laughs as if they are laughing together, and she reaches out and squeezes his shoulder.

GRAFTING

The monk is so giddy he can't take a step. Across the barn, hot with aromas of piss and lupin, the shepherd is bent over, laughing with his friends. His eyes are so sad, the monk moans quietly and wipes foam from his mouth with the back of his hand.

A dozen villagers stand around, supplicating him with their tales. There are no high-growing fruit trees, but Mopsus Peter has a devil tree so tall the highest ladder in Plainfield cannot reach the bounty, and when pears fall from that height they explode into poofs of pear that soak the ground, so the tree feeds upon its infants and grows higher. Corn, berries, rye: all of these require attention and are tamed with much expense of labour. "We are Boolavogue's first defence against nature's infinite face. Everything you eat comes from us. We are inside you."

Near the shepherd, the dairymaid sits on a table next to a bowl of figs, still as a pin at the centre of a top. Men in clean trousers cascade from her in a ring, dancing to the loud fiddle music, slapping each other on the back.

The outrageous necklace sitting on her chest glitters like a trout, contributing to his sense that she is half-fantasy. The monk blinks. Those diamonds cannot possibly be real—if they were, she could buy three villages with them. Other women have decorated themselves with baby's breath, violets, ribbons, and lace. The dairymaid's necklace is a bright tear into another world. It draws her in, swallows her. The monk blinks again. He sees her unsmiling face, but it immediately slips into the necklace's aurora.

POWERS

As the barn swells with music, and the men and women stomp on the pale oak floor, the shepherd blows the fiddler a kiss, she wags her tongue at him, and he throws back his head and howls. But he is too aware of his actions to lose himself in the performance. The shepherd watches the monk watching the dairymaid. Winking at the monk, he takes the dairymaid's hand and pulls her off the table. When she resists, he pulls harder.

The shepherd kisses the dairymaid's neck and pushes her by the shoulders to the man across from him, who kisses the dairymaid's cheek and pushes her by the shoulders to the man to his right, who kisses the dairymaid on the lips and pushes her to the man across from him. He grabs her waist and the back of her head, dips her down, down, kisses the tops of her breasts, shrinking from her necklace as if from a sun. His friends howl. The shepherd looks up at them and laughs. He picks her up, sets her on her feet, and presses her into his body, slowly twirling out of time.

Rage swamps the shepherd's blood.

So she is already far away. She has abandoned him to the darkness of the woods. He is a shepherd—he knows abandoning a creature in the woods is the same as killing it. But she cannot go so easily, he will not let her. He will follow. He will scream at her heels until she turns around. He will grab hold of her with his teeth.

REGRET

The dairymaid sways against the shepherd. She is lost in another world, the one over his shoulder: the world of self-flagellation. Now the monk knows, doesn't he? He sees how everyone hates her, how the men touch her. She's disgusting. But why did she invite him tonight in the first place? Had she really been naive enough to dream that if he came, and they were here, together, she might become a different person?

The dairymaid presses her face into the shepherd's chest and thinks of the jewellery box with the little white bear, back in their cruck house.

She will work through the night, she will bring the monk her butter when she goes for her lessons tomorrow. She thrills at this possibility, always on the horizon, of showing someone the truest thing about herself, something she made. Of course, the shepherd has tasted her butter, as well as some of the cheeses she has started aging in their shed.

Her eyes widen, the barn's stained floor rushes at her. She thinks of him spreading her latest creation of lemon and leather onto a piece of bread, taking a bite, saying, "Good, babe," and slathering the rest with jam. The shepherd is a loyal and beloved dog she has taken into the yard and shot between the eyes.

Suddenly she grips his arms and looks up at him. "I love you."

She kisses his mouth, his chin, his neck. She clings to him and kisses his cheeks. "I love you, I love you," she begs.

The shepherd drops his arms. She will never forget his face at this moment. Her frantic pledges die in her mouth. In his unblinking eye she sees the depthless dark. He knows she lies to him. The dairymaid flushes. He does not understand the complexities and subtle layers of butter tasting, but he knows her.

SIX YEARS AGO

On days when the shepherd does not return to the boulder in time to save a lamb from the wolves, he punishes himself by staying out all night in the fields.

The mother ewe's terrible loneliness makes her affectionate, though already she forgets why she is sad. She cries out into the night, staring at the darkness of rocks as if to ask, did she ever have a lamb? But the shepherd is real. She presses against her darling in his low leather cot, which he carries with him at all times for days like these.

He rests a hand on her rump. The stars are white as bones. Every quarter hour, he wakes to stare at the pricks of light, and wonders: are these holes in a curtain that blocks us from a magnitude too awful? He lets his eyes hang open and follow constellations of their own devising. His senses know a secret logic. Shapes reveal themselves. A horn growing out of a woman's puckered mouth, a goat with hind legs that trail off into spindly infinities, lines upon which he wills convergence. But no. Parallel lines will remain an exact distance apart. He arches his back as though to bend his spine is to heal the bald fact of lines, but his shoulder blades will never touch. He stares and stares, light years into the distance, and feels like he is floating in a void.

Back in the village, the dairymaid will panic for him. She'll see horrible visions of him dead, injured, or—a dark consolation—she'll imagine he abandoned her, he is a betrayer. She'll mourn. She will recover. Move on. Moment by moment, she will get over him.

BACK

Enough. Without releasing the dairymaid from his eye, the shepherd steps back, leaning so his arms hang at his thighs. Enjoying the flexibility in his shoulders, he clenches his jaw and smiles at the dairymaid through bared teeth.

Ancient wrath seeps from the shepherd. It is so easy for her to lose herself in whatever she does, in whoever she loves. For him, it's the opposite. The more he drinks, the more he jokes, the further away he stretches above the other shepherds and dairymaids laughing up at him.

He laughs, and a dozen people laugh around him. As though attached by thin red strings from their chests to his fingers, he holds the need of his friends to find certainty in an entity larger than themselves. A pack.

One shepherd after another joins him in his backward walk, until a dozen of them surround the dairymaid. He hates the pitying, repulsed look in her face. He lifts his chest and howls, and the shepherds laugh, stomp, clap their hands, and then they all howl at the dairymaid. They throw back their shoulders and catapult howls at her. Knuckles white, faces red, they give all their breath.

One of them steps closer, and the circle tightens. A hand swipes at her. Three more hands reach for the dairymaid, and then the clasp at the back of her neck breaks, the band bends open, and the dairymaid's seven diamonds fly into the room.

She holds out her hands and screams.

Yipping, the pack of shepherds fall on them, and then the dairymaids, like rams cresting a ridge, throw themselves between the shepherds until the whole junket is rooting through the tangle of hands for the immeasurable riches.

The shepherd watches the dairymaid, her hands reaching forward, and he sees why they hate her. It is not that she was a girl-bride, and their powerlessness in the face of her assault makes them feel like cowards. It is not that she reminds them of how their sons and daughters might be taken from them at any moment and sent to the battlefield or to a lord's bedroom. It is not her vanity. Nor do they hate her for not sharing her diamonds with them.

They hate her because, through some perverse arrogance, she will not spend her wealth—not even on herself.

He confesses to himself that he hates her for the same reason.

POLITICS

The monk shakes off the miller's hand and pushes his way into the ring of howling men, but not before the other dairymaids descend upon them and shove him out of the way. When he looks again, the dairymaid is gone. He spins from side to side, searching for her.

Behind him, the barn doors swing open and the junket is slapped with a lashing of rain. There stands the lord's vassal in a black cape and pantalets. He nods at the monk as he comes in, unsticking a grey strand of hair from his forehead with a long fingernail. His presence casts an aura of ambiguity across the party. The music speeds up and presses into a happy chorus line that repeats its mounting pressure without resolution. Then it just stops. Couples break apart, allowing the vassal to pass into the centre of the barn.

The lord's vassal takes the scroll from his breast pocket, cracks the wax seal, and reads the names of those drafted for this year's war. "From Fitzramford, Lord of the Vassalage of Vanderwater, including the villages of Plainfield and Roslyn. Harry Softhorn. Pete Drindle. Dorrow Spieler." No voices moan or cry as he reads on. Twenty shepherd boys and one girl. Dominique.

"*Domine Deus, Agnus Dei*," the monk mutters.

He digs his nails into his palms. He is the only one here from Boolavogue, which it is the army's duty to protect. He does not condone how things are done. Or does he? He bows his head. Next to a table leg glitters one of the dairymaid's diamonds. Quickly, he bends and puts it in his pocket.

When he stands, there she is in front of him. Her dress is torn, her arms crossed over her breasts. Four claw-marks swell on her chin and across her shoulder. The monk squeezes the diamond in his hand, it cuts his palm. Her cheeks are red, her eyes black. He has an urge to tie her to a pole and bring her to the Inquisitioner, only such things have not been done for hundreds of years, and he finds the thought repulsive. With a flush, he pictures the screw, his face in the mirror, the nerves in his testicles, the blood around his navel.

Between them is something like a bright rain—of hope, of a mutual desire to disappear into each other and hide—that is too much for him.

"Why do you stay here?" His voice is more contemptuous than he meant it to be.

"Because it's my home." She frowns and turns to go. "Because if they want me to leave they can chase me out."

DAWN

The shepherd had lain awake on the dirt floor of his sheep pen amid his ecstatic flock, who watched over him in the night, listening to the submission of rain against the canvas flap strung to four posts. Had she really not come looking for him? Not even out of fear, out of loyalty, out of the concern a stranger might have for a person who is self-imploding and forlorn? No—she did not come.

Now, as he walks with his ewes, the woods glisten, sodden and cold. They have not yet shaken off the night. But the chickadees and finches shriek in celebration for another morning. The sun has risen! The sun has risen! One day it will not! Through the trees, the river is ablaze with rapid light.

As the shepherd approaches the heart of all this terror, he glimpses a shape among the ruins of Honeywell Shrine. He stops. His ewes stop.

There is the monk, in the shepherd's own secret place, crouched over a slab. His face is pale, his beard flat on one side, as though he woke early and came directly to this place from his bed. He is holding up a white sheet and running a nub of charcoal over it. An acorn drops from one of the great oaks and bounces off the monk's shoulder. The monk glances away from his sketch. In a gesture both casual and familiar, he picks up the nut, pops the top off with his thumb, and tosses the body into the grass.

AT THE TEMPLE

They're here, the shepherd and his flock, bursting from the forest like a rapture.

"Your face!" cries the monk.

He watches the shepherd reach up to feel, not a chin, but a black-bearded promontory of bone. Horror sweeps the shepherd's eyes as he buries his hands in his new mouth: the thin, stretched lips, the thick tongue, the teeth. A snout grows up the shepherd's cheeks. Hair emerges from his face as though each of his pores is a bowel.

The monk howls his blessing. Let him make the sign of the cross! Let him drive the devil away! Has the shepherd found a cursed mask and dared to put it on?

The monk blushes. Even in the midst of his terror he hopes this is the case and knows that it isn't.

The shepherd runs to the river, falling on the bank, staring at his reflection, and when next he looks up at the monk, his eyes are divided, blue at the top and amber on the bottom, horizons on the edge of wheat fields.

And through all this, don't the monk's hands tingle with the exhilarating release of guilt? The shepherd is no soft-hearted innocent, therefore the monk has no real authority to misuse—this is beyond what he knows.

"*Salvum me fac*," cries the monk on his knees.

The shepherd watches him with his great wolf head. Then he pushes himself to his man's feet and walks into the woods, followed by his sheep.

LESSONS

Shrunken, pale, reeking of bitter soap, the dairymaid jiggles her foot against her high-backed chair. The monk has never been late to the library before.

Around her rises a vortex of books, rung with stairs, terraces, and ladders.

I am a bubble of green, she thinks.

She scans the ocean of possible worlds, brass labels over burgundy spines, seeking a place to rest. But the tower pushes her eyes higher, into the small circle of black at the top. She winds the key of the music box in her lap. The little combs ring out in the silent library. Under the lid, the bear twirls.

NECK

The monk stands at the library door, watching her. The magnificent magnitude of the room collapses into the impossible slightness of the dairymaid's neck.

"You," he whispers. She turns.

"Will you come upstairs with me?"

Her eyes are black and sharp. "Yes."

She follows him through a small green door and up the narrow stone stairs that spiral around the lavatory chute. Climbing, listening to her footsteps, he is in shock. He pushes open the door directly off these back stairs, into his tiny stone room with its shard of a window, useful only for shooting arrows through. He has done it. He has brought her up the stairs like he has dreamt of a thousand times.

He feels himself resolve into a point, he has no thoughts, he is a shot bullet. Quickly, quietly, he takes the box from her and puts it on his small table. Then he lifts his robe over his head, watches her flinch at the scar erupting from his navel like a painting of a dying star.

She neither makes a secret of her fascination nor shies away from this intimacy by replacing it with a tamer one, say, by looking above the scar into his eyes.

For the first time since childhood, the monk feels that he is revealing the truth of his loneliness. Only now, he does so without humiliation. Nothing that happens now is an accident.

Except for one small thing.

When the dairymaid rolls her head to one side, the monk is, again, struck by the delicacy and loveliness of her neck, and feels, suddenly, a wave of mourning. Will he never again see her neck from this aspect? The monk buries his face in the dairymaid's neck and experiences a secret moment of terror.

TWINS

The monk's youthfulness, his beauty, his crystalized angles, his resolution and shyness, leave the dairymaid with nothing to say. She clings to him and stares with amazement at his shoulder blades rising like heron bones from his back, as he presses his face into her neck.

And the dairymaid thinks, this is what twins must feel like in the dark, growing in the plenitudes of themselves and encountering one another, interplanetary solitudes. How can a twin ever be happy once it has been born? How can it get over the isolation that lasts for the rest of its life?

In the Genesis story, the monk has told her, lies something more than a story. There is a lyric, a cry.

The story is that everything was once together—and then it came apart.

The cry is that, after coming apart, all the particles are still hurtling in the direction in which they were flung. Always in shock. For all eternity, astounded and awake.

PASTORAL

Sometimes accused of indulgence, of glossing over injustice by idealizing poverty, pastoral is also an elegiac mode, resonant with lament for a lost connection to nature, to family, or to elemental rhythms. William Empson defined pastoral as any work that contrasts simple with complicated life, including in his definition the proletarian novel, or the narrative written from the point of view of a child. Often it accompanies—even in the pen of the same author—a turn toward epic, the genre of war. Perhaps in the guts of every soldier

and his ravaged wife, in the anxious hearts of every administrator and her neglected partner, in the guts of all the adults
complicit in the injustices of their nation and work, lies a
pastoral. It is the elaborately artful genre that cries, *Once, we
were good!* It is a mode well suited for broken hearts.

GETTING TO KNOW EACH OTHER

It is only after they make love, when they are lying on his cot
under his single candle, that the monk inhabits the naked
ideal of himself: generous, modest, insanely hopeful in the
sublime face of meaninglessness.

With the dairymaid as his audience, he says, "Loneliness
is the condition of my love," and "Love is intensified by the
prospect of death," and "I live with one half of my body in
death," and, warming his hands on her breasts and thighs,
"This will haunt me for the rest of my life."

"Why?" she says. "Where are you going?"

He looks down at her. Her expression is calm and cold.
He frowns. "The miller told me. About your past. I am so
sorry. It must be self-alienating to be both yourself and a
function of a rite of defilement. It isn't right."

"You're very analytical," the dairymaid says. "It's reas-
suring."

He touches her face, disliking how little it reveals of her
thoughts. "You have to stay here, with me at Rahab. It's
terrible, how they all are. And your shepherd's part of it,
even though I feel pity for him, too. He's just a shepherd in
a village. Still, he has choices, doesn't he? He's still a moral
agent. Maybe you could clean the rooms? Then you'd have a
reason to come up here, or I could visit you secretly at night."

She stares at him unmovingly.

"Or something else you'd like. Maybe you could do your churning."

She stands, takes her butter box, and falls back into bed.

"Will you try this?" she says.

"Of course." He swallows.

She winds the key, and in the dimness they watch the bear twirling to its sad chimes.

Shyly, he dips a finger into her butter and puts it in his mouth. It is very good, very fresh. He tells her this. She smiles.

"Maybe I could make butter and the monastery could sell it."

"Well," he says, "the monastery already sells the beer it manufactures from grain the villages tithe it. But I'm sure you could talk to someone in charge, you could tell them how the butter's done. Other people do it, you know," he whispers. "Other monks bring maids."

She nods stiffly, which annoys him. Aren't they used to affairs like this, these people of the world? "I have to go to evensong," he says, rising into an understanding that his freedom to leave this room, when she is trapped, is a kind of violence. "I'm sorry, I wish I didn't have to go. Will you be okay here?" He puts on his robe.

"I guess I'll find out."

In his pocket, the diamond weighs on his thigh. Remembering it, he takes it out and hands it to her. "This is for you," he says.

She looks at it.

"I found it. Last night."

She sinks her head into her hand.

He blushes. "Last night must have been very hard."

"Oh must it?" She snaps her head up and glares at him. "Weren't you there?"

"It's not like a diamond isn't a tempting thing to keep. I thought about keeping it."

"But I earned it?"

"But it's yours."

She nods again and takes it from him. "Thank you for the generous tip."

It is a small moment, when he feels himself float above his body and say with cold delight, "You're welcome."

He shuts the door behind him and exhales into the darkness of the stairs. His heart pounds. He pities the dairymaid, but pity, he thinks, is the price he will pay in exchange for the pleasure of hurting her.

DISCOVERY

After a few hours, the dairymaid learns it is as easy to leave the monastery as it is to enter it. She stands on the clay path that winds from the monastery to the village, watching the blood-orange sun descend into the forest. Now here's an evening to make you glad for your life.

As she ponders this marvel, the old temptation arises to picture both the monk looking down from his stone window and the men of the fields looking up from their labour, and to fantasize that their yearning converges upon her, as the sun fattens her lips and burnishes her shoulders in gold.

But immediately she wakes up from this fantasy of worship. No one is looking at her, nor should they be. She must go. At night the hills and pastures are not safe from things that live in the ground. As soon as the sun disappears behind the tops of those trees, I will run home, the dairy-maid promises herself.

Her stomach lurches. She pictures the dimming light of the tower, and the beauty of the monk's face, its slightness, its youthfulness, its angles.

But then, as though her mind contains a rotating wall in an old castle that spins her not into secret passages but great halls, she finds herself before another image: the shepherd's blue eyes, his red cheeks, his laughter, the flowers he hands her, his impotence.

It seems to her that the wants of the shepherd and the monk are principles that can determine not just events in her life, but her reality and all her perceptions. Free of their desire, she might stand here forever and look and look, and time might diminish its hold on her.

But then the final, furious flame disappears behind the tallest oaks of the forest, and the dairymaid runs, lungs burning, heels bruised. As though the woods have detected her flight, they start to howl in all four directions, advancing their territory over the night.

As she approaches the boulder that marks the final bend in the path around which the lights of the village will be revealed, the dairymaid sees a large, hunched figure emerging from the trees. Her heart flings itself against her chest when, in the grey light, she recognizes the shepherd's cream shirt and brown pants. She stumbles to a halt.

He stands at the shocking threshold where fields vault into forest—staring, the dairymaid realizes, at a crying lamb. But though his eyes are his own, wide and blue as a summer sky, his jowls are elongated. Hair runs from his temples to the corners of his stretched, black lips. He sniffs the air, looks up from the lamb, and sees her.

The dairymaid looks into his terrified blue eyes. Then she runs toward the village. He chases her.

FENCES

He lopes at the dairymaid's heels, sniffing her ankles, snapping at the hem of her dress. She only thinks she is running away. The hardness of her pounding blood, her breath, her sweat—it is like a plate of cheese before a holiday feast. His torso is a cavity of air surrounded by iron, his paws skim the ground as lightly as tossed stones, his mouth is a meticulous instrument, and every nerve is under his control.

They pass the stile into the village. Her pace slows only slightly, she would not even know she had slowed, she would not have registered relief.

Shouts clap around them. Along the fences marking off the lanes, villagers run and point.

The dairymaid runs into the green in the centre of the village, runs in a circle with the knowledge reaching her too slowly that she is alone.

Other shepherds rush to the scene, but they stand back and swear, they clap their hands, not hiding from each other how excited they are for this show.

She is spinning around and around, trying to see him, but he is spinning with her, always at her heels. He clenches his amazing jaw. It could snap the femur of a deer.

Suddenly, something jabs his side and knocks the wind out of him. The top of his snout erupts in pain.

The other dairymaids stand above him, beating him back with their churning poles. Their braids whip around, their faces, against the clouds, are elated.

The wolf slinks between their legs. Shaking his head to dispel the pain in his snout, he turns to look at her, bent over with her hands over her face. Good enough. He saunters down the village path back to the woods. When the other shepherds run at him and make a show of trying to kick him, he easily dekes away.

PHYSIOLOGY OF THE BLESSED

Toes ringing, thighs and testicles chilled meats, nipples hard little stones, body sending thrills of minute alarms—the monk crouches at the side of his empty bed.

When he imagines the dairymaid deciding to leave his room, the back of his head buzzes with spirited tentacles seeking the darkest, coldest depths of the sea. The time has come for him to accept that, even in love, he is best suited for being alone with himself.

People bore him. He trembles to admit it. Only with distance and formality can he relate to others—when there are rules, and schedules, and a defined role for him to play. He thinks of the dairymaid's delicate but vital neck, with its salt and veins, and pinches the top of his bare foot with the nails of his thumb and pointer finger.

It is shameful to have a body, and so it should be, for the resurrection is directed to the final perfection that is contemplative life. If the risen continue to eat, the monk recalls William of Auvergne asking, in due course of time, won't Paradise just be full of shit?

DARK

The dairymaid walks alone through the dark village.

She feels excitement for the immensity of the woods, the full moon hanging over the black colossus of the monastery, the stone towers jutting skyward like formations of the earth created during a distant apocalypse.

At a future time, when she tells this story, she will emphasize that it only took her twenty minutes to walk to the other side of the monastery, further than she had ever gone on her own.

Did anyone try to stop you? people will ask.

It will always be hard for her to admit that no one did. The dairymaids had given her a cloak, new shoes, three loaves, and a bladder of water. She'd walked along the row of them as they sent her off, looked into the round, incredibly smooth faces that they moisturized constantly with butter. They touched her shoulder or patted her hair or kissed her own buttery cheek. Now that her diamonds had been absorbed by the village, she had become one of them. They wished only the best for her.

Once she reached the border of the vassal lands, she set off down the highway, past low fields of dirt that had been razed long ago. In the distance before her, she saw first the moon, then a tiny blue lantern approaching swiftly.

When she shares this story later, with sympathetic Boolavoguians agitating for the closure of the vassal lands, she will always pause to tell them: "And I thought, as I stood aside to let the wagon pass: the girl in there is excited. She'll think the majesty of the horses corresponds to something great and unique in her. *I am entering the world*, she'll think. Never mind that it's night. She'll think, the world is large, but easy."

HOPE

The wolf slinks after the wagon, up the hill to the lord's castle. Bouncing on his paws, he darts from one side of the road to the other. When the wagon passes through the lord's iron gates, the wolf waits until the gatekeeper closes them and returns to his shed. He pushes himself through the bars and moves across the dark, sparse grounds, from hedge to hedge.

For such a large, many-towered fortress, the door to the lord's castle is small, made of thick planks of wood rounded at the top. The brass knocker is made for a larger door—a man could not lift it with one hand.

The wagon sits on the cobbles, empty, with its door open. The white horses in their blinders bob their heads stiffly, but do not stomp or whinny or fret their lips. She will be inside, hunched over in a blue cloak, warming her small feet.

In three years, when it comes time for her to leave the lord's castle, she may be tired of the love of men. She, like the last dairymaid, may not wish to go abroad. Then she will come to him, he will take care of her. When everybody else looks at her aslant and talks in mocking whispers, he will be the only one to bring her flowers. They will never make each other feel ashamed.

He lifts his head and howls long and low.

She will hear his howling and know he is with her.

Every night, he will keep the new dairymaid company until she is free to come to him.

DAIRYMAID

Many years later, the dairymaid is hanging a wheel of raclette over the counter of the fromagerie she now owns. Through the open shutters, she watches her daughters prance up and down the street in hats her friend has given them to play with.

"What's a milliner to do with four sons?" her friend wails, though actually her sons model the bandeaus and flowered bergères just as happily as the dairymaid's daughters. Children prancing in fancy hats is one of their street's charms.

The girls tiptoe by with their hands flat out at their sides, waggling their bottoms, bowing at leashed dogs, gaining easy laughs from the passersby who have come to the old part of the city on this golden afternoon, one of the last of the summer.

These are some of her friend's more fountainesque Gainsboroughs—as her daughters mince along, bright peacock feathers and cut ribbon spray people nearly in the face. But alas, these hats are failed. Her friend's sons had left them on the pavement to set just as it had started to rain, and now periwinkle and garnet dyes have converged upon the brims and turned them the colour of bog.

"To frolic in the sun wearing errors on our heads," says the fine-featured father of the dairymaid's children, who is beside her, pencilling damasks onto the paper they will use to wrap cheese.

She grins. They are close. They work together. They have planned for years to write a poem.

Yet they also struggle. There is still a need for small formalities, or they too easily descend into bad indulgences of spite, for the distance between them is always there.

Perhaps, thinks the dairymaid, that kind of family ease—the naturalness of a secret language, the faith that it is all as regular as the holidays—can only happen once. It is good. Their children feel at home.

A high, elegant wagon clatters to a stop on the cobbles outside. The wood is black and sleek, but now that the wagon is stopped, one can see pale nicks where the lacquer has chipped. There are blotches of robin's egg blue on the sapphire curtains pulled taut over the windows where the sun has bleached the silk. The white horses are young, but look closer: bloody gum flecks their cheeks, for they have been ridden hard. In fact, it is their speed upon which the wagon's grandeur depends.

Her husband snickers, as he always does at vanity, and goes into the back—an agreement they have reached because he, unlike her, is incapable of putting on a happy face. His honesty is bad for business.

But the dairymaid is not thinking of business. She has gone silent as the past.

You have been waiting your whole life for this, says a low voice inside.

And here he is in her doorway.

Fitzramford. The lord of the village of her youth.

He is liver-spotted now, grey and spindly except for the paunch that holds his swollen organs. But his lips are the same. Fat as leeches, and loose, as though they do not care to touch his teeth. They are the kind of lips that vault easily into a sneer or bend into an O of pleasure, lips that seem to be made of a more aquatic flesh.

He nods at her with a palsied timorousness, mutters good day, and smiles with every attempt to hide his stained teeth, which embarrass him, before limping to the bowl they keep on the counter full of the rinds and ends of cheeses—a bowl of scraps ideal for melting down into a mongrel roux.

And the dairymaid realizes it is not just age that has humbled the lord, or sickness. Nor is it the past: his eyes pass timidly over her face without recognition or interest.

It is simply his parochialism.

He nods again and blinks in the direction of his wagon, as if to say, all these rich but decaying accoutrements, he knows they are laughable here. The puff tie so out of fashion. The stale cavalier vest, brocaded tailcoat. His accent, which seemed so proud in the village, now sounds provincial.

"A nibble for my pet cat," he says, dropping his handful of fromage on the paper she has slid across the counter toward him.

And the dairymaid remembers: the stately blue light in the wagon, the curtains always drawn, she believed, to hide her face from the profane eyes of the world. The grandness of pulling into hotels at night, of rushing up the back stairs draped in a satin cloak, music on the balconies from the operas, the smoke and rare meats and fine liquors.

She had glommed to it, to the feeling of men's power—had mistaken the secrets it keeps from the home, its home-lessness, the secret that she had been chosen, mistaken it all for her own private invitation to the great world where she too might glory, unburdened by care.

She remembers the things he'd specially brought her in tiny packets, and her taking the pieces of dark chocolate and smoked pork belly and rank cheeses so carefully in her hand, smelling them to show him her sophistication, her bravery, her willingness to savour something of an acquired taste. But all of those morsels were cheaply bought, she now knows. Nobody else ate them.

"What about for yourself?" says the dairymaid, in the theatrical voice she uses with customers. "Don't look surprised—we've got the same accent, see? You've come a long way, and I know what it is to be in the presence of a lord, even if here it's only a game we play. Happily, I am not in a position to deny a little hospitality to a fellow countryman, and anyway, you wouldn't miss an opportunity to sample some of the best cheeses on earth?"

The dairymaid goes to the display case and fills a small wooden box, walking past the lord, who—distracted by the hanging wheels, the chutneys, the loaves of bread in baskets—realizes too late what she intends to do. But he cannot stop her. He is old, he limps, and she is still young, strong.

She is, she sees with immediate sadness, in the prime of her life.

The dairymaid opens the wagon door. Inside, the girl starts, but only slightly. She is tiny, white, and smells of musk. Her hair is unwashed, her nails black. She is younger than the dairymaid's own daughters. On her tiny crimson bodice are the dried stains from where the lord has allowed her to spit. But her expression is proud, expectant, though there is a wrinkle of confusion to be faced, all of a sudden, with a mother.

"For my lady," says the dairymaid, as she hands the girl a box of her finest, rarest, most delectable cheese.

THE GAMINS OF WINNIPEG

ONE JUNE NIGHT IN 2016, a meeting of the gamins of Winnipeg took place. Of course, the meeting began after midnight, in the French part of the city. No, these gamins weren't children, if that's what you're thinking. They had all prevailed into middle age, residing between the ages of thirty and fifty-eight.

They sat at a cluster of small round tables under the zigzagging iron stairs and screened-in balconies behind the Nicolette Inn, more a tenement than a hotel. A light hanging from a telephone pole yellowed the sharper points of their faces but left all their roundness obscured. They chose this location because they liked to be surrounded at all times with structures that reminded them of their youthful nightmares. When they turned their greasy, cropped heads east toward the train tracks, they could observe on the horizon the huge barrel that held water for the abattoir. Elevated on three spindly legs, it looked like an iron virus. Closer, in a park behind a chain-link fence, stood a weathered statue of the fourth-century Assyrian martyr, St. Febronia, its face blacked out by a cloud passing over the moon.

They all suffered under the particular wavering of gamins: confused by the world's righteousness, while at the same time committed to the serious absurdity of their own dark souls. But recently their suffering had increased. They were under attack—or, at least, that's how they saw it.

They were being put to work in a coat factory. Even at a thirty percent employee's discount, the gamins couldn't come close to affording coats like these, stuffed with real goose feathers and lined in fur that had been dyed Tyrian purple using the secretion of a predatory mollusc.

Of course, the people putting them to work thought they were helping the gamins by giving them an opportunity to earn a living, and maybe even the life purpose of a vocation. These philanthropists didn't know gamins already had a life purpose, which was to exist on the razor's edge of survival, getting by on their wits alone, never lifting a finger. When it came to work, the gamins practised conscientious objection. In their opinion, laziness was ethical.

But now the kitchens and walk-in clinics and even the shelters had closed, in exchange for the gamins getting work and registered housing. The nation demanded gratitude.

So, that night, after eleven hours spent plucking the feathers from the chilled corpses of gutted geese and tearing the tails off rabbits, the gamins gathered to discuss how they should meet this assault on their liberty.

"We could burn down the factory," Helen said.

"Might as well set yourself on fire," Kay said. "The next day they'd put us to work somewhere worse."

"I want to live in a tree," Tommie Queenie said.

"Nobody ever asks my opinion, but why don't we open our own residence again here in the Nicolette and employ ourselves?" Delilah said.

"Too old for brothelling, never liked it," said the gamin who for many years had gone by the name of Chappie. She was the most muscular and the ugliest of all the gamins, and their leader insofar as that was possible. Every gamin was a histrionic. Even Chappie, ugly as a devil, was no exception.

"Oh, the world'll use force—it'll reach inside and play us like puppets," Chappie said. "But the power to stay useful to nobody and nothing is ours until death. Sure I'll go get my paycheque from a coat factory, if that's what keeps me alive, but what I'll really be doing—and there's nothing they can do to stop me—is living a contemplative life. I'll pluck and think, pluck and think. But I won't pluck much. If they want to reform me, they'll have to cart my hog-tied body to the people who give lobotomies."

Chappie didn't look at any of the other gamins as she spoke. She had turned her chair away from the gathering of small tables to face Febronia's statue. They all knew it wasn't rudeness. It might be said that Chappie was in love with the stone Febronia—not a day went by that she didn't visit her. And it was at Chappie's insistence that the gamins had met by Febronia's statue at the back of the Nicolette. While the coat factory growled for them like a greedy gut across town, many of the gamins suspected that, more than stuffing coats, it was distance from Febronia that strangulated Chappie's soul.

Deeply committed to strange, irresolvable passions, the gamins lifted under the anger in Chappie's voice. All except for one: Chappie's daughter, Lene.

For a long time now, Lene had known that the only way she could give herself over to the gamin's pledge—of uselessness, insolvency, whimsy, artifice, and profitless philosophical speculation that offered consolation to everyone's soul but hers—was by being drunk. Lene was the most manic of all the gamins, the loudest, and the biggest prankster. Before the coat factory, she'd spent most of her time at a busy intersection pulling antics. She especially liked to wobble into the busy streets and moon traffic. Motorists dropped money in her can just so she'd get back on the curb. *I don't need your crushed ass on my conscience!* they shrieked. Sometimes she pretended to jump off a bridge just so drivers would crank their heads and smash into the back of another car. Other days she sat on a hard, wooden chair with her hands on her knees and silently wept, and if anyone stopped to look at her, she slowly met their eyes and sang "Rock-a-bye Baby."

But despite her constant giggling, in her heart Lene knew she wasn't really an impish embodiment of the chaos principle. She had no impulse to keep the universe on its toes, to provoke its creative retaliations. No, Lene had the soul of a nihilist. She was obedient to the silent call of the vacuum. Faced with the inevitability of death and annihilation, Lene stretched out her arms and dreamt of speed. She felt love for all the tiny, fragile things, but in the end remained loyal to the direction of time and to mortality. If Chappie was the heaviest gamin, Lene was the smallest and the lightest.

Since she began going to work with all the other gamins at the coat factory, a strange thing had happened to her. Lene discovered she liked sobriety, so long as it was paired with utilitarianism—and that was because utilitarianism was its own kind of drunkenness. The slow conveyer belt snaking from the roof of the warehouse down to the ground, and the gamins perched at each level on a series of stairs, each tasked with plucking her portion of goose and tossing the feathers into a metal suction cup that shot them into a sterilizing vat beneath the floor: these activated in Lene the same thirst for inevitability that a twenty-sixer of rye would.

More than anything, Lene hated the lazy, ponderous nonchalance of the gamin who did not nakedly pluck her section of goose. And the worst, laziest offender was her mother.

So at the meeting behind the Nicolette, Lene stood up to present her idea, sulkily vaping a cloud that smelled of coumarin pipe. "Actually," she said, "Delilah's onto something with her brothel idea. We have to make our own money. That's the only way to freedom. But instead of brothelling, why not our own factory? Consider the muff. Everybody knows the most useful thing for a gamin to own is a muff to keep her hands warm in the frigid winters. That way, when the mood strikes, her fingers can limberly clutch her can of paint."

All the gamins nodded; gamins were famous for spraying illegal murals that spread the surreal quality of their souls across the cities in which they made their homes.

"Of course, none of us gamins owns such a muff. But be honest. Which one of us, sitting on a curb in winter with our hands frozen stiff between our knees, hasn't itched to paint? Our souls sit dormant and unexpressed for at least six months a year, especially at this longitude! We can't be our own customers, nor can we rely on the gamins of other cities to keep us in business, seeing as we're all so cheap. So I suggest we make muffs for highly functioning, well-paid normates who wish they were gamins. At the coat factory, only the rabbit's tail fur is used, to line hoods. The rest of the rabbit gets taken next door to the dog-food factory. Gloria, Billie, Oscar Medusa—you're going to filch pelts. Tommie Queenie—you'll drain off some sterilizer from the vat. Helen, Kay—you'll steal upholstery scrap, needles, and thread. The rest of us are stuck plucking geese. But at night, we'll make the muffs. Then in the summer we'll all dress up in our most poignant attire and walk around the streets in our muffs, setting the trend. Come fall, we'll sell them at the farmer's market in West Broadway."

Most of the gamins began to whistle and meow, excited by Lene's proposal and the opportunity it gave them to be magnificent. But Chappie said, "Aren't we here to discuss how to get out from under an arbitrary obligation? Why would we invent another obligation?"

And just like that, with a collective sigh of pity and, perhaps, built-up resentment—for a long time, Lene in particular had considered Chappie's dedication to a life of contemplation, really a dedication to a life of contemplating Febronia, to be a pious and self-righteous affectation—Chappie was toppled from her unspoken role as head of their ragamuffin collective.

Now muffs drizzled from the grey sky of Lene's sober imagination, tantalizing her with their bitter, monotonous oppressiveness.

❦

To market their muffs, the gamins invented an Ideal Gamin.

The Ideal Gamin was grotesque enough to be interesting, but possessed the waify, unintentional beauty that would-be gamins liked so much. The city responded to the murals rising up all the bare, brick walls of the Exchange as if tickled awake by an ancient wish. The many identical faces of the Ideal Gamin bore such radiant rebelliousness, everyone who looked at her shrugged a burden off their shoulders and felt all the paranoia of their lives fizzle away.

The teenagers of the city's wealthy residents started hanging around the intersection where the gamins used to stand before they went off to work at the coat factory, and they began spray-painting their own variations of the Ideal Gamin in her long, folded gowns, her hands hidden in deep pockets.

The city celebrated this new atmosphere of debonair irony. The streets became trendier each minute. So many people gathered to practise sophisticated absurdity. They stood on their beds giving spontaneous at-home poetry readings inspired by guests' blood types, formed hundred-person circles and hook-knit collective tapestries, wrote out names backwards in menses, summoning long-dead political rebels. The city became obsessed with devotional practices, so long as everybody's devotions made a great spectacle.

Even Lene's original plan to steal rabbit pelts and other material proved unnecessary. The owner of the coat factory, David Thompson, an ambitious and impressionable man named after the eighteenth-century cartographer, fell in love with Lene, and she agreed to marry him. He bought the dog-food factory next door and transformed it into Lene's muff factory. He even followed her advice in turning the coat and muff factories into co-ops, so the salary of each gamin immediately quadrupled.

The country fell over itself, enchanted by David Thompson's moral transformation at the hands of a gamin. Every other city began to look toward their own gamins for untapped potential. Soon every citizen believed that the initial prodding to work had activated in the core of the gamin population a hitherto unsuspected creative energy.

But Lene's success only brought her unrest. Every day her eyes fled across the shiny, productive surfaces, and away from the busy, contented, increasingly well-fed faces of the gamins proudly plying their trade. Always, her eyes landed on Chappie.

If possible, Chappie had gotten even uglier over the last two years. Her grey hair receded bluntly around her head until it looked like a wool face cloth dropped over a newel post. Her eyes, always small, now seemed invisible from across a room. Her cheeks were red and inflamed and had too many swollen folds, as if her face had diaper rash. She'd lost a few more teeth, all in the front, and every few seconds she had to give a good, long suck so she didn't dribble. Her bottom lip hadn't had any feeling for a while.

Not once did Chappie lift a finger toward the composition of a muff. It was all they could do to get her to pluck a goose. And there she failed as well. Sometimes she would stand stock-still and stare at the conveyor belt, fixated on a stain as it moved slowly, slowly, slowly along, while her goose went by untouched.

To top it off, Chappie became pretty much mute. Her silence didn't seem hostile, though. Once, her son-in-law took Chappie aside and explained to her how usefully her talents might be applied toward the painting of marketing material. Chappie yawned and said, "I think I'd like to paint the bottom of a lake."

Lene took Chappie's laziness personally. Whenever she looked at Chappie staring at a spot on the belt, not working, she would feel a tug backward, toward a hunger for the good, honest life that had always terrified her. More than anything, Lene did not want to be duped into a state of hopefulness.

Every day at three o'clock, she watched Chappie stand on the street outside the factory, her shoulders slumped and a content, an absent look on her face, waiting for the bus that would take her across town to the little park, and to Febronia. One day in February, Lene herself stepped outside the factory, looked both ways, put up the furred hood of her long coat, and crossed the street.

All the smoky nights of Lene's youth rose up around her like a chorus of ghosts: the subtle speculations made

over bottles of wine as candles burned; the dusky sky like a
Venetian painting announcing to her child's ears, *Here I am,
a sad illusion owing my existence to you.* The stories her hideous boyfriends told her lying on her mattress in the dark
as, over their scarred and bony foreheads, she would catch
a green flash of the northern lights out the high clerestory
window—stories about how they had resigned themselves
to their ugliness and deformity by finding a body to worship.
Pity is hard and even revolting, Lene concluded back then,
but it is a kind of love. The only kind that could distract her
from herself, when such distraction was what she sought.

She knew, now, as she walked toward Chappie's dark
eyes, that she was temporarily moving in the direction of
the past.

"Hey, Ma. Let me drive you."

They got into Lene's new Telsa, went east, and parallel
parked. They walked across the flat field of ice and sat on
the bench. In this park, far away in centuries and space
from Febronia's fourth-century Assyria, her statue had
been doodled on by children and pissed on by dogs and
men passing through. Two Xs blacked out her eyes. A
piece of hockey tape gagged her mouth. A plastic shopping bag with something used and bloody in it fluttered
in the wind, hitched to Febronia's elbow. Middle-aged
pigeon shit stained her head and shoulders. It was as
if human capriciousness had joined with the forces of
nature to humiliate her. Not even Chappie, who loved her,
ever cleaned her up.

Lene had always called Febronia Chappie's girlfriend.
But as she sat there with her mother in the cold that day, she
admitted to herself that she always hated Febronia because
Febronia was like a better, less manic daughter to Chappie,

one who calmly endured the anxious delirium of the world.

Lene put her crow-coloured head on Chappie's shoulder. "Ma, back when you used to paint, your murals were so full of impossible longing."

She said this knowing the time was coming when the world would no longer seem alien and surreal to her. Soon, she would open the front door of her little century home south of the river and feel, for the first time in her life, the comfort and normalcy of the family and possessions waiting there for her return. On that day, the roof would close and she would be trapped in an immeasurably small yet engulfing abyss of her own making.

When Lene raised her head again, she was angry. "What is the point of a person like you? Why don't you do us all a favour and let the axe finally drop? We know you hate your life."

The expression on Chappie's swollen red face was as cheerfully impassive as ever. "You know I haven't done anything to hurt you, Lene."

But Lene was hurt. For, in fact, the first painting of the Ideal Gamin Lene had ever sprung upon the city, and the one that had completely beguiled it, was an exact replica of this stone Febronia: the same starkly staring eyes focused on a radiant complexity in another world, one more worthy of Febronia's attention than the clenched jaws and wide eyes of her Roman tormentors. Up the grey side of the Richardson Building, it was Febronia's image that leaned against the handle of a shopping cart, with her hands—just like the statue's—buried deep in her pockets, as if clutching hidden talismans.

It was as if Lene had taken upon herself the task of exalting Febronia, for Chappie.

"Why don't you just kill yourself," she advised. "Then you won't drain people dry with your total lack of interest in anything other than this statue of a make-believe martyr."

‹‹‹‹›››

That night, Lene couldn't sleep.

Chappie had seen Lene at her most pitiful and cruel. Mothers know something about daughters that daughters don't themselves know. No other intimacy in Lene's life came close to matching it in intensity.

In the morning, she rushed to the coat factory. Thankfully, Chappie was there at her usual spot, not doing much. Lene was relieved that the worst parts of her nature hadn't wounded Chappie as much as she'd feared. But she was also annoyed with herself for simpering around Chappie that day, complimenting her ludicrous rubber boots and professing that she had always found Chappie's dreaminess inspiring.

Lene's obsession with her mother only grew after that.

She thought Chappie a fake, and she wanted to scratch apart her mother's pretensions and get to whatever lay beneath. Lene began to berate Chappie on the assembly line in front of all the other gamins. Whenever Chappie came out with one of her homespun pronouncements—things like "We are like cacti. The deeper the winter, the more shocking the little red flowers in summer"—Lene threw back her head and rolled her eyes in disgust. She shuffled behind Chappie and her hanging lip, and criticized her mother's hair, her nails, and her weight, as well as her failure to be a strong, self-sufficient role model.

But with every vengeance, Lene felt lonelier and lonelier.

Eventually, she could think of only one way to pierce Chappie's self-sustaining heart, and to make her know that Lene was really there in all the magnitude she felt was her experience alone. So she petitioned city council to remove the statue of Febronia from the park behind the Nicolette. "It's so degraded, it's a disgrace to her memory," Lene argued.

One day, at the end of June 2018, Febronia's statue disappeared. Workers power-washed the pedestal on which Febronia had stood for who knows how long, in preparation for whatever would go there next.

None of the gamins had intervened when Lene told them, one at a time, with a sadistic glint in her eye that felt almost like an offer of camaraderie, that she was off to petition city council. But when Febronia's statue went away, they immediately suffered a collective stab of remorse, and then a flutter of panic as their hearts tried to run backwards in time. That day, silence presided in the coat factory as they all gave Chappie a wide berth. No one had the courage to tell her that Febronia would not be there when the bus pulled up to the park. Next door, the muff factory buzzed with pronouncements of innocence.

Just like that, the gamins turned against Lene. They said they'd been beguiled by a prodigal daughter. Everyone patted Chappie's shoulder when she left for the bus that evening. They squeezed her hand and gave her little smiles.

From behind the coat factory's glass doors, Delilah pressed her garnet-coloured head against Oscar Medusa's tiny, malformed ear and whispered, "Are we murderers?"

Oscar Medusa rubbed his hands all over his face and shook his head. "I don't think I can be here," he said. "Tomorrow I won't be able to look her in the face."

The next day, fewer than half of the gamins arrived at work. Chappie, however, did show up. Everyone looked at her carefully, as if just the force of their eyeballs would be enough to shatter her like a plate.

Eventually, at noon, Helen said, "How are you feeling today, Chappie? Are you okay?"

"Fine," Chappie said. "How are you?"

"Meh," Helen said.

Chappie stood at her station, plucking the odd feather and staring off at nothing, just like she did every day. Because they sympathized with her so much, and because they wanted to lie at her feet and grovel for forgiveness, the other gamins mimicked her behaviour. And all of a sudden, as if their eyes shifted to allow a buried image to emerge from a hologram, Chappie—who had looked so hideous and alien to them these last two years—became familiar again. So familiar, in fact, that the other gamins thought of themselves as younger, more handsome variations of Chappie.

Due to everyone's laziness, production at both factories shuddered to a near halt.

"What? Do you really think so little of me?" Lene addressed the banditry of black-and-red-haired gamins when they confronted her in her large office with its rooftop view of chemical release flu-gas stacks. "I have a wonderful surprise, actually—a very expensive surprise, if you'd like to know—that I wanted to give my mother next week on her sixtieth birthday. It's Febronia that Chappie loves, not some old, pissed-on statue. Just you wait."

The gamins became terribly excited for Chappie's birthday. It felt like an opportunity to make kind and extraordinary gestures that would redeem their past behaviour. "Thank goodness for birthdays," they said. "Whoever came up with the idea for birthdays was a genius in group psychology."

Lene organized an enormous party in Chappie's honour in the basement café at the Nicolette Inn. There were gimlets. There were pastries cooked over a live fire, pea soup poutine, a room in which to dance, and a room in which to sit over cognac and have a political discussion. A woman, dressed in a rabbit onesie with the flap open at her butt, played an electric piano. There was a movie screen showing a film about legless nuns flying away from a war in hot-air balloons, but getting blown back onto the battlefield. In one corner sat a little hive on a table with bees flying all around it, to remind everyone of the sting at the heart of festivity—the gamins found this touch a bit tired and avoided the area. There was everything Lene hoped Chappie would like. But the party was one hundred percent a gesture of hope. Chappie was impossible to buy for.

All night, Lene hovered by Chappie's elbow, barely able to keep the final surprise to herself.

Finally, when the room had gotten dark and vapoured, and all the gamins were dancing slowly with their arms over their heads, pretending to be anemones waving in the currents of the sea, Lene took Chappie's dry, swollen hand and said, "Come on, Ma." She pulled Chappie across the dark parking lot. All the other gamins followed. They awkwardly climbed the fence, catching their emerald-green nylons, and clustered around the bench, taking pictures of Chappie with their iPhones and posting them to Instagram. Not one gamin had the courage, in that moment, to look up from her phone.

Before them rose a restored Febronia, a shiny white marble Febronia elevated on a clean pedestal, her hands out of her pockets and raised before her, as though she no longer needed the talismans to comfort her.

"She's glorious," the gamins gasped, staring into their cameras and snapping pictures.

They really needed the new statue to be glorious. And objectively, there was no denying her preciousness. This Febronia was made from bone-white Calacatta marble. A twenty-four-karat gold halo reigned over her head on a little metal post. Her sad eyes, two huge, round opals, were so pure they radiated starlight. She was so valuable that a chain-link cage had to be locked around her.

Chappie sat on the bench. She crossed her legs. A smile quivered on her face, then disappeared as she tried to restrain it. But she was not looking at Febronia. She seemed instead to be watching the moon.

Seeing Chappie so ungrateful, Lene's mouth filled with bile.

"Nothing?" she said. "I went to all this trouble just to make you happy, unlike anything you've ever done for me, and you have nothing to say?"

Chappie turned around and peered into her daughter's anguished face.

"Lene, my dear," she said. "I've never really told you about Febronia, have I? I waited for you to ask. You never did, so I kept her to myself. I didn't want to impose her on you.

"It's a true story, as true as stories of saints and martyrs can ever be. You can google it. Back in the earliest days of the fourth century, Febronia was the niece of the abbess Bryene at a monastery called Daughters of the Covenant, at Nisibis, Assyria. She'd lived at the monastery since she was two. At eighteen, she had grown so charismatic that whenever she read to the public, which was often, they immediately understood complex, abstract forms that had previously been opaque to them.

"In 304 AD, in the heyday of the Great Persecution, Diocletian sent his generals into Northern Mesopotamia to torch the monasteries there. Everybody fled to the mountains—all the monks, most of the nuns, and, at the front of the pack, the bishop. But Febronia stayed back. Her aunt Bryene stayed with her, and so did one other old nun, a woman named Thomais, who recorded this story. The Roman prefect, Selenos, renowned for his brutality, took one look at Febronia and offered to spare her if she renounced her faith and married his nephew, Lysimachus, who was one of the soldiers present.

"Febronia refused to renounce her faith and to marry Lysimachus, and was sentenced to excruciating torture. Her hands were bound and a yoke set around her neck. She was led outside, stripped naked, and tied to a tree. Her teeth were smashed, her tongue torn. Her skin was flayed from her back. Her hands and feet were cut off. Her breasts were cut off. Only beheading put an end to her suffering.

"But it is said that she never cried out any of the confessions of guilt the Romans wished her to say. The only words she uttered were, *Stay with me*. In the end, Lysimachus was so affected by the brutal torture of someone so powerful, he immediately gave all of his worldly possessions to the new monastery they built right after.

"Sometimes I would sit here and marvel at the degradation of Febronia's statue. I wondered at the rude drawings on her body, the garbage that stuck to her, the piss staining her robe. I have always thought of Febronia as a gamin, even though gamins aren't usually religious. It struck me that all the abuse the statue of Febronia endures, all the ruinations of time, only amplifies its power.

"And now you've knocked her down and replaced her with a better version of herself, so she can't even be missed. I think that perfects her: removed, thrown out, supplanted, forgotten. You really are my daughter. This is an excellent present."

At that moment, Lene understood that her own real mission had been to eradicate the gamin spirit wherever she found it—not out of hatred, but from the fear that attends a great love.

She stood in brief silence, in the cool black of this northern park with its few witnesses. Then she took a tiger lily from her hair and placed it, through the cage, at Febronia's feet.

"Now she's remembered a little bit," Lene said, glaring over her shoulder at Chappie.

Chappie smirked.

Lene bounded up, threw herself onto the bench next to her mother, and rested her head on Chappie's lap. After ten minutes, it felt less humiliating. After twenty, Lene's eyes filled with tears and she felt, for the first time, no longer young.

EMBASSY ROW

AT FIRST, YOU COULD SAY, OUR MARRIAGE WAS GOOD, considering our fathers had arranged it one night in the Emirates back when we were preteens. Our starter home was a state-of-the-art monolith on Embassy Row. Those fledgling years, we ran around its multi-function rooms naked, watched Netflix until dawn, hosted pool parties where, drunk on gin, everyone skinny-dipped in the blazing water lit with blue and red bulbs as our banter screeched into the preternaturally huge, solid-iron fence that surrounded our property to shield us from the world.

After a conventional exploration of orifices, sex with my husband all but disappeared, popping up every four or five months with a desperate, vengeful attitude, scatological and extreme. He and I liked to make dares—that was interesting.

There were quieter, soulful times, too. One rainy day in the Hague, we lay on a hotel bed imitating each other's faces for hours.

His was round, like the moon.

"You look like a talking pie," I said.

"And you have a small Adam's apple."

That's how the joke voices came about, the noises we'd make to end arguments—through mutual revulsion we found hilarious. We were endearingly sadistic to one another.

And when my father finally died, my husband sat on the edge of the tub, holding my hand as I writhed through bitterness, and then sorrow, for the respect I hadn't inspired from that freckled swagger of a man—my dad. But at the wake, I laughed. People kneeling behind us put hands on my shoulders because they thought I wept.

Sunday mornings, we'd wrap ourselves in the nostalgic hum of the refrigerator and bake lavender delights. We had no children, so we spoiled each other instead. No innocent third party, not even a pet, nothing living, should come between us and our every passing desire. Nothing should curtail our freedom, we said—especially my freedom, I said.

꙳꙳꙳

One day, I pulled through our mammoth gate and found my husband whipping our lawn mower. Despite the uncanny racket of his yelling and the motor's whine, I made sense right away of the whip. It was an heirloom only our closest friends knew about; he'd inherited it from somewhere antebellum and extinct, a blot along his paternal line. His semicircular jaw was so flexed that his face looked like it had been removed and then pinned back on. Behind the madly swinging lever of his body, our desert willows were shocking in their stillness. It was as if someone had cut out the elaborate shrouds of dry fuzz with a highly specialized machine and hung them in the air.

"Who do you think you are, boy?" my husband shrieked, cracking his whip. Spit flew out of his mouth. "You ain't got no family and no religion. You just got to work until you die."

My main concern was that, somehow, a neighbour or passerby would see. I was afraid. I was ashamed. Leaving the lawn mower running, I dragged my husband inside and put him in a bath.

Hours later, as I moved from room to room, clutching my hair as if I were my own blond, decaying doll, John Deere choked out there all alone in the night. I did nothing to relieve the jagged arcs of silver cut into the paint.

ॐ>>·<<<

Our parties took a morbid turn. All of us on Embassy Row, not just my husband, began exalting over our possessions with invincible contempt. Instead of frolicking buff in our pool, the men stood around its perimeter, jabbing the water with barbecue skewers, pulling down their trunks every now and then to urinate on its spangled surface. We wives clustered behind them at the tiki bar and gulped gin by the truckload. We whipped martini glasses into the cement. "Clean it up!" we screamed at the veiled maids.

It wasn't disgust that kept us huddled at the bar. It was, finally, requited desire. We wives loved each other on those nights as if we were the flesh of each other's flesh. We wanted to leap off a cliff together into a black lake. We wanted to commune on a living heart. Instead, we drank gin and smashed glasses.

The mornings after, my husband and I would wake at noon, acidic and pinched, to berate each other.

"When you did that 'erotic dance' last night?" my husband said.

"It was just a joke."

"It looked...really bad. I don't want my friends to feel sorry for me. Would you consider a labiaplasty?"

"We'll get ourselves in order," I promised. "We'll relandscape."

But then our weed whacker coughed up its last fume of gas.

My husband, he lynched it to the birdfeeder with its own cord. He linked up the rakes and power-washed them until paint bled off their handles. Then he chastised the power washer for being too aggressive by backing over it with our new lawn mower.

I went inside to get him a drink, but really I watched him from the kitchen window, to admire from a distance his vast geometrical stature. I plugged in the toaster, then unplugged it again.

"Hilary."

I yelped. *Here* was my husband, right behind me. How long had I been staring at an empty yard, at the tired heap of glinting machines?

He grabbed my shoulders and spun me around. I threw back my head, opened my mouth for the toaster cord he strung around my face like a bit. I whinnied with a terrible thirst possible only in a land of infinite dunes, and gave myself up to the high noon sun. Outside, our bright, golf-course-quality grass screeched with its own greenness. Not a shadow on it, not from the fence, not from the house.

He was rough, but not rough enough. I found him shy, a coward. And I was a coward. We couldn't look each other in the face. I had to shut my eyes to scream as loudly as I wanted, and even though I had nothing to lose, I still didn't give it my all.

⇥⇥⇥⇤⇤⇤

Soon the Franklins found someone to sell us black-market DVDs, and our parties moved from the pool to our home theatre room. We stared hungrily between the bars of our fingers at an oven in a cement room being dismantled by a masked man. When he unscrewed the door, we gasped at the redness of the coils. No one told us they would be hot.

Maybe it was a long-desired distraction from the wars. We were diplomats, all of us, from various United Nations. Suddenly we were throwing up our hands. We were fed up with war, fed up with peace. But we weren't tired, no. Our parties became more frequent now that they were indoors. They ran later, spilled into weekdays.

With his tongue, my husband pressed the button on the remote that controlled our floor-to-ceiling Roman blinds. As he watched the shades unfurl themselves and fall in total abjection, he quivered with a longing we'd never had for each other. Eventually I'd say we needed different blinds. He would stare at the floor and mutter proper, righteous sentiments regarding cost and waste.

The more preoccupied he became with our drapes, the more outrageously I craved black-market DVDs. It was the same with all the wives. Veiled from the world by blinds I hated, we gathered to watch illegal footage of stripped and gutted appliances in our entertainment room. The men, less interested now than they had been, took habitual trips to the kitchen to refresh their drinks and, we knew, steal long, probing looks at pictures of drapes on their phones.

We wives were thirsty all the time. We drank cases of gin. One night, we swarmed the kitchen. We edged closer to my stove, dripping martinis, clutching at drawer handles to prop ourselves up. For a moment I felt a surge of guilt for the baking I used to do and shouted, "No, not mine," but the wives pushed me out of the way and dragged my stove into the garage. One at a time, we stepped forward to twist off its knobs. We didn't unscrew the oven door; we wrenched it off and threw it to the side. We popped the glass top away with a cutter. We picked up shovels and, squealing like a litter of pigs, jabbed them in and out, tore dents in the gas tubes. My stove wobbled on its stainless-steel frame. We left it there, three quarters undone, for days.

After that, we found it hysterical that people still warred. We drove to the edge of our properties, poked the controllers that opened our gates, and watched the thin pillars of smoke fade weakly into a colourless sky. It shocked us how pathetic war looked in real life. All we wanted was one single cloud to bleed exuberant fire, but nothing that spectacular ever happened.

We sought out wreckage to drive our SUVs across. It was the only reason we still left Embassy Row. I would wrap my arms across my husband's chest as he drove, staring into the side of his wide, exhilarated eyes, catching his laughter, gasping as our Hummer jumped sharp hunks of cement twisted around rusted pipe. I would put my hands over his hands clutching the wheel and know our old, beloved joke noises couldn't compare to that adrenaline.

When I wasn't giving myself up to the hot, shrieking high of it all, I missed our lazy afternoon swims, the warmth of cuddling under a towel with a glass of port, the hours spent in the kitchen baking, and even the original pool parties, the innocent, naked dives we dared each other to take, our first years of freedom.

But you don't notice warmth in this kind of heat. Those remorseful feelings passed.

Back in our driveway, we hosed off the Hummer. No force will take glass out of tires.

~~~~~~~~~~~~

Despite the suicide bombers and drones, it was never a problem getting new appliances delivered. We left everything on all the time. The noise, the whir, and the taste of metal, the blood running across my husband's chin when he clamped down on hunks of electronics I'd prepared on a platter—well, no country hike or trip to the mall compared to the outer-space height of our new life.

Still, addicted as we were to amplification, every now and then we mourned for something sweet, or felt the impulse to console. When my husband found a black kitten mewling around a checkpoint, he stopped the Hummer—disdaining the land mines slotted at random in that casino of dirt—and brought the tiny, resilient thing home. Hardly anything survived out there in that dusty, alkaline air.

How gentle were my husband's hands when he placed the kitten in my arms?

That first night, before the unstoppable current of guests arrived, we rested our faces in our cat's fur. He didn't have fleas or worms or a tail. Suddenly, here it was: our third party, our common love. But we couldn't name him. Instead we begged him, "Tell us who you are. How did we find you, you of all the possible cats?"

"And who is *this*?" our friends gasped.

"We can't decide," we confessed.

They tittered at our whimsy, then barged in with their usual asphyxiation. In all the mania, however, we remembered to take care, each one of us, to pick up the kitten whenever he tiptoed his small, callused paws over something sharp.

As weeks spun by, we gauged their passing by the weight he gained and the increasing plushness of his hair. He followed our parties to the basement, where we'd taken to smashing computers with cricket bats. Nothing bothered him, not the noise or sudden movements. He would jump from the hope chest to the tray carried by our decorative serving boy to the plasma screen's precariously thin lip to a high shelf where we kept big things that wouldn't fit in the kitchen. Even when all I wanted was to be borne away by the vandal in me, I couldn't ignore him. None of us could. He was a garrulous mewler. His noises sounded like unbiased journalistic questions: *Why what how?*

With thin pliers, we plucked tiny silicon transistors off of circuits, ten at a time, like nails from a baby. My kitten moved his head back and forth, back and forth, over the identical prongs scattered at random on the floor. To me they gave no answers, but I was convinced he deciphered arrangements only an outsider could perceive. We watched his cratered green eyes for signs, saw glare from the overhead light. Someone gasped, "Is it spring already?"

I lay in the grass one day, staring up at the pale sky past the high black surface of our impenetrable fence. The sky did not seem at all to be past the fence, but next to it, as if sky and fence were two solid halves of a flag.

My kitten came and sat on my chest, purring. I stroked his head and whispered, spontaneously and for the first time, his name. A knowledge of wholeness and of home made my spirit swell, and I felt like I might actually be a part of this desert place. I could hear the faint bleating of the struggling life here, of the translucent insects and the imported grass.

The feeling subsided. I sat up and looked down into my kitten's face. I thought my heart would break if I stared any longer at just the tip of his pink tongue.

"What did I call you again?" I said.

꙳꙳꙳

Soon the indoors bored us. Our parties moved back outside to the pool.

One night—a hot dancer of gin and poolside gleam and the dry, red remainder of a desert sun—I found my husband standing tall as a flagpole beside the diving board. A rocks glass in his fist trapped the lights strung around the pool and turned them into cubes.

He made a sound like a body dropping on sand. All he said was "Oh."

My kitten's tailless rump bounced off the side of the pool. His face was wedged in the skimmer, his tiny wet paws curled in on themselves. Someone—my husband, bless him—turned down the music.

I picked up my kitten, resisting the thought that earlier, was it me who said he could swim across one of his nine lives while we laughed and laughed? Only it wasn't my kitten. It was a bunched-up black cotton dress, the one I'd been wearing. I threw it at my husband.

"It's just my clothes, you idiot!"

My husband poked the heap with his toe. He stomped on it.

"Stop it," I said. "Where *is* the cat?"

We looked, of course. We did a thorough job of looking. We turned on the floodlights and searched every corner of the yard, under the chairs, behind the bar, in the pool shed, clacking our tongues or hissing. Our fences were high, our gate shut tight, but we could not find him.

In the days and weeks that followed, our neighbours called to report sightings. From their third-storey windows, they claimed to have seen a sleek form bouncing happily or murderously or coyly or anxiously, depending on who was calling, along the top of the fence. *On top of the fence!* we marvelled.

Often, I sat alone in my kitchen, staring at the saucy void where my stove had been. I imagined my kitten would be up there on the high black fence, looking across rows of identical brick cubes, unable to discern one house from another. Was he afraid? There are no birds for him to eat, no grasshoppers. He must hunt the lizards, his only company.

If only I could remember his name. Then he would understand me when I called him, he would recognize his home, and me, his friend, among the identical residents of Embassy Row.

THE PARACHUTE

The writer's only responsibility is to his art. He will be completely ruthless if he is a good one. If a writer has to rob his mother, he will not hesitate; the "Ode on a Grecian Urn" is worth any number of old ladies.

—William Faulkner

IN AUGUST 1941, while convalescing from a severe bladder infection at her villa in Berlin, Leni Riefenstahl discovered an essay written by a certain Emile Novis.

She did not come upon the essay herself—lonely work! Not that she could, in any case. The essay had originally appeared in the December 1940 issue of the Marseilles literary monthly *Cahiers du Sud*, and though Riefenstahl was indeed the White Fairy, a genius of cinema, she did not read French.

What happened was that Riefenstahl's art director, a well-schooled woman named Isabella Ahland, had called from the telephone box on the set of Riefenstahl's stalled adventure film, *Tiefland*, which was shooting in the small Bavarian town of Krün. Isabella—best described as one of those fresh-faced ducky blondes with perfectly styled middle-aged hair and constantly applied lipstick, the ones who look as if their parents have friends who work for national magazines, and in fact, her uncle Ruetz was an editor for *Modenschau*—had, in order to entertain her maestro in her illness, translated the Novis into German, and was reading to Riefenstahl from her notes.

On its own, Novis's essay, "The *Iliad*, or, the Poem of Force," was nearly powerful enough to make Riefenstahl feel as if something had drawn her to the ceiling and entangled her in a large chandelier.

But the real pleasure was that Isabella was reading it to her.

Without an audience, Riefenstahl ceased to exist in her own eyes. Though she always threw her proud body and soul into her work, the pleasure she took from this absorption was one shared only between her and the muses. Her artistic struggle still required a human witness. She had always known this. It was the result of her striving toward her fate under the jealous guard of a tyrannical father. Remove the tyrant—Alfred Riefenstahl was at this date aged and decrepit, three years from death—and the path to fate opens too wide.

She hated being alone.

And the truth was, Isabella had become Riefenstahl's best friend. Yes, Riefenstahl had other friends—she was not a woman who got on only with men. She had friends that extended all the way from her youth: Hela, her roommate at school. Hertha, with whom, at twenty-one, she had travelled north to the Baltic Sea. The young Jewish banker Harry Sokal, who had financed her first dance recitals. But now, at this high point in her life, she rarely saw the companions of her youth. They existed for her like the gods to whom one prays. At Christmas and on their birthdays, she mailed them extravagant gifts, as if paying tithes.

"Director, I must use the toilet," Isabella said, breaking from Novis.

"Hold it," Riefenstahl commanded.

Isabella did so, aware that Riefenstahl treated her own bladder infections as if they were playful choices made for a bit of theatre—that, as a child, Riefenstahl had imagined a tiny dwarf perched on a stool in her bladder, stabbing her with his thin needle. But though Isabella liked possessing all the intimate details of Riefenstahl's bladder pain, she, in turn, did not want Riefenstahl to know about her Crohn's, or her stoma, or the fact that the little piece of intestine doctors had hooked through the incision in her pelvis was ten centimetres long and red as a puppy's cock. She knew that Riefenstahl hated sickness.

Riefenstahl said, "Isabella, did you know that if a man turned his head to me on the street, my father would pinch me and say, 'Your toes, slut. Watch them.' But the second Vati moved away, I would smile at the man with mouths for eyes, like the fox in the coop."

"No one could manufacture a childhood like yours, Director. It's why you're an artist."

Isabella continued reading. When she came to the part in Novis's essay about Justice's twin, Nemesis—the dark geometrical god who brings destruction equally to all sides—Riefenstahl sat up from her mustard chaise and leaned on her elbow.

"What does he mean—'Nemesis is the soul of the *Iliad*'?" There was a look on her face that suggested she had an affection for horror. Despite her forty years, Riefenstahl had the air of a child, unhearing but wide open—an air aided by her uncanny eyes, which were just millimetres too close to her nose.

"Well," Isabella's voice crackled over the line, "he means that Homer is an impartial narrator. If he shows a soldier on one side being killed, then in the next scene he will show a soldier on the other side being killed, and the vengeance continues back and forth. Homer could be a Greek or a Trojan."

Riefenstahl sighed. Isabella was young, ambitious, quick—and completely inexperienced in film. She didn't realize that Novis's argument contradicted Riefenstahl's aesthetic.

The White Fairy had only one subject: beauty. The gorgeous, strong, and victorious. The banner hanging from a sky. The hale maidens with downcast eyes and wheat in their hair. All the freshly bathed youth, flung by a trampoline with their naked chests open to the dawn. The statue that comes to life and runs naked in all its blond animal love down a Greek mountain past eternal fires. In essence, Riefenstahl's films were not impartial. She was a German at the start of the Thousand-Year Reich: she looked forward.

Homer, on the other hand, could look back.

"Isabella," Riefenstahl said, "you will find me this Frenchman, Emile Novis, at once. In him lies my solution."

"Solution to what? *Tiefland*?"

"*Tiefland* is a shitting piglet. *My* solution, Isabella. The solution to *Penthesilea*." She glanced down at the shadow of the telephone cord on the carpet and quickly pulled up the tie on her kimono.

"Director, I insist on permission to use the toilet."

"In the Greek myths, you'll recall, Achilles kills Penthesilea the Amazon queen on the battlefield outside of Troy. Only when he removes her helmet does he realize his foe was a woman, and he falls in love with her corpse, perhaps even commits an act of necrophilia. But in *my* version, Penthesilea is a woman who loves a man, Achilles, and kills him. She tears him apart with her teeth! She is a beautiful brute, pure desire and instinct. In the union of Penthesilea and Achilles, life and death come together. What they form, only for a moment, is, is—"

"Love?"

"—power. Real power. Like the creation and apocalypse unfolding in a single instant! Ah, what is power but the ability to ruin something large? But I have lost the way with *Penthesilea*, Isabella. I know it is my masterwork, it will redeem all the errors of my life, but I am beginning to fear it will never be made."

"Nonsense," Isabella snapped. She admired Riefenstahl more than anyone in the world. "You are Leni Riefenstahl and I give you my vigour and youth. If it's Novis you need, I will find you Novis."

Riefenstahl yawned. She stared into the mirror over the desk where her telephone sat. She scanned the room behind her, examined a moss-green drape and an antique Japanese folding screen with silver paintings of what could be hairy kittens or terrier puppies or dragons. She flicked her eyes down, in case the terriers crept off the screen and turned into scorpions on the floor. Bouncing blobs of sunlight seemed to dance across the woven roses of her rug, but she knew in truth they were devouring colour. She pressed her cold pack to her eyes.

Isabella spoke again. "I guess that was a bit actressy. Sometimes I like to pretend I'm in one of your films." She then paused and said weakly, "Director, honestly? I'm about to crap my pants."

"You will hold it," Riefenstahl said.

⇒⇒⇒ ⇐⇐⇐

At exactly that moment, 1,540 kilometres southwest of Berlin, Emile Novis puffed across Marseilles in a black worker's jumpsuit, high black socks, black boots, black hat, and round, black-rimmed spectacles. She was walking from the flat on rue des Catalans, where she had just been arguing with her mother, to the attic offices of *Cahier du Sud* in a building overlooking the Old Port.

To a whimsical observer across the street, she might have looked like a little choo-choo train, her eyes—magnified by her thick glasses—as helpful and terrifying as two headlights on an actual train emerging relentlessly from a tunnel a ways off. She was supernaturally thin, with rotten teeth, and radiated a strong feeling of the inevitable. People liked to look at her, partially because she inspired relief that they themselves had not been crushed yet.

Her real name was Simone Weil. Due to the anti-Semitism of Vichy France, even among the largely progressive readership of *Cahier du Sud*—a prejudice that had just seen her and her brother André removed from their university teaching posts—the director of the quarterly, Jean Ballard, had asked Weil to write under an alias.

SIMONE WEIL
EMILE NOVIS

It is an absurd life when an editor says, "Discover an anagram of your name," because three of one's grandparents had set foot in a synagogue.

Now brother André was moving to New York, with her parents to follow—and after the events of the day, they were after her to join them.

That morning, she had woken at four o'clock and practised Sanskrit for an hour, then spent the next hour helping fishermen collect trash along the docks. She then went home and wrote a poem, which she read to her friend

Jean, who always came up to the apartment after his morning swim. Next, she stopped by Lanzo's flat to review his plan to start an intentional community in the manner of a French Gandhi. Then she and her Catholic friend Hélène went to Dominican House, where she told Father Perrin about the month she'd just spent farm labouring in Saint-Marcel. To her delight, she was so rejuvenated from chastising her body with physical work that she felt none of her usual revolted mesmerism when he dabbed mucus from his continually inflamed left eye onto his robe.

The police were waiting for her when she returned home. They were there because she'd filled out an application to join a resistance group, in hopes they would get her to England so she could start a league of front-line nurses. When, at the station, one cop called her a little bitch and threatened to lock her up with the whores, she had vanquished him by lighting a cigarette and remarking, creamy as custard, "I have always wanted to know that environment and I can't see a better way than going to prison to find out about it."

Her parents, who she found afterwards crying in a café next to the station, didn't care that the police had found her unbreakable.

"If I say, 'Come to America,' you get on that boat with us," said her mother, Selma, back at their house on rue des Catalans, with its sunny views of the sea. "You can organize your league of front-line nurses in New York. In New York you'll have real friends."

"In New York I would fall into utter despair," Simone said, pausing to press a strand of tobacco from the cigarette she was rolling into the gums above her front teeth. "Do you think I could abandon everyone here to the most significant event of our lives, then come back and just pick up where we left off?"

"Why do you hate your family?" Selma said. She lit a strand of her dark hair on fire with her cigarette and put it out with two wet fingers. Then she began to cry for the second time that day, an unheard-of occurrence, and not without joy for having a daughter who was a warrior. "God, you scare me, sparrow. You're so skinny."

"Being self-disciplined is the most—"

"What, you want to be perfect?"

"Of course I want to be perfect."

"That kind of ambition is so safe."

Weil's heart pounded. She knew Selma was right. Maybe it was not self-discipline but self-honesty that was the most philosophical act of all. She had not been honest with herself. Yet Selma, who puffed on her cigarette with a victorious flash in her eye, did not know of Weil's most recent commitments. Her writing, her work—yes. Some of it was good, and she had the strength not to publish any of it, to walk with self-knowledge into oblivion. She could lead a different life of perfect courage.

Weil propped her foot on a wooden chair, took the notebook from her deep black pocket, and wrote: *Fear of missing out is the real reason I don't want to go to America. All my friends will bond together under adversity and they'll forget I ever existed. Weakling! Yet I must not go. What does it matter what energy or gifts there may be in me? The same is true of others who do not have the option to leave.*

Then it was four o'clock, time for her daily visit to *Cahier du Sud*.

꒚꒚꒚ ꒚꒚꒚

When she came into the offices of the Marseilles quarterly, out of breath from climbing the stairs, the two green-eyed Jeans—Jean Ballard and Jean Tortel—scattered from the settee to the bookshelves along the edge of the room. Ever since they had started making her write as Emile Novis, she terrified them. Or rather, their complicity terrified them. They really were on her side, but what else was to be done? The world had become, as everyone frequently said, a theatre of the absurd. They felt this most in her presence. When she wasn't there, life stopped feeling like a dream.

"I was arrested today," Weil said to Jean Tortel, the poet, who had put her in touch with the English resistance group and now stood pressed into a bookcase. "That means there is an informer."

The telephone rang, and Jean Ballard, the director, answered it. "You want to speak to Novis?" Ballard said into the telephone.

"You can stop glaring at me, you psychotic man of the sea. It wasn't me," Tortel said, pulling a book at random off the shelf and flipping through it.

"It's for you," Ballard said to Weil in a campy German accent, his hand on the receiver. "It's a Berlin ferret asking to speak to Emile Novis, writer of 'The *Iliad*, or, the Poem of Force.'"

Ballard then joined Tortel against the shelves, taking the book from his hands and flipping through it himself, squinting at the pages. "So who do you think the informer was, then?" he asked Tortel, as Weil marched across the room and took the black receiver.

"Could have been her, for all I know," Tortel replied. "She's one of those people who will sit there quietly reading a book at a party just for the attention."

"Tell Riefenstahl I'll do it," Weil said loudly into the telephone. "On one condition."

"*Riefenstahl?*" the Jeans said.

"Involving a plane and a parachute."

"I knew it," Tortel said. "Self-informer."

➳➳➳⋖⋖⋖

Three days later, Weil gave Selma's grandmother's pointe native ring to the owner of Cinéma du Soleil de Marseilles so that she could sit in the theatre alone all afternoon to watch Riefenstahl's *Triumph of the Will.* Afterwards, she went to the warmly lit lodgings of her dear friend Simone Pétrement and sat smoking in an old orange armchair.

Pétrement interrogated her from the canopy bed. "Has anything passed your lips today?"

Weil theatrically swallowed her smoke in response.

"Gross."

Weil blew exhaust trails of smoke at the picture of the Virgin by the window.

Pétrement took a brown bowl of blackberries from a walnut side table and brought them to Weil. "Take a berry."

"I don't want a berry."

Pétrement poked Weil lightly in the eye.

"Ouch," Weil said. With the thumb and pointer finger of her left hand she took a berry and pushed it between her lips.

"Take another one."

"Very well."

"Another one," Pétrement said, cupping the bowl of berries in both hands with her arms straight out.

"Good God."

"More."

"I'm full."

"Impossible. More."

"Here, look—I've eaten the bowl."

"No—that one fell on your lap."

"Fine. Here it is. See?" Weil put the last berry on her tongue and, holding it in her mouth, continued to smoke. She looked up at Pétrement in her white nightgown, dark hair springing every which way, with the bowl in her hands. *She looks so sad*, Weil thought.

"Come here," Pétrement said.

"No. I have to write my analysis of Riefenstahl's propaganda film." Weil flicked on a green lamp and dragged her notebook from a satchel onto her lap.

"Are you really going to jump out of that plane?"

Pétrement was referring to the fact that Weil had agreed to meet Riefenstahl on the following condition: Riefenstahl was to fly her to occupied France in a German airplane, so she could parachute into the Compiègne Forest north of Paris to join the liberation forces. Riefenstahl was also to provide the parachute.

"I love you," Weil said. "But no one on earth can stop me from doing what I want."

"Who are you talking to when you make those kinds of pronouncements? It's not me." Pétrement knelt in her nightgown on the green rug before Weil. She put the bowl in Weil's lap and a hand on each of Weil's slight shoulders, then drew her close and pressed her right eye to Weil's left eye. They blinked, batting lashes. "My inclination in this matter is a commandment of God," Weil said.

Isabella was sure that when she called Riefenstahl back with the information she'd uncovered about Novis, Riefenstahl would laugh and say: *Close the lid. The monkey is dead*. First, she'd found out Novis was actually a Jewish intellectual and activist named Simone Weil, opposed to the Reich *in blood, apparently*, and not just ideologically, spiritually, politically, morally, and aesthetically. Then, there was the absurd condition Weil had given when she agreed to meet with Riefenstahl, the one regarding the parachute.

But Riefenstahl said nothing. Instead, she looked at the yellow bouquet her Führer had just brought her, along with a special nostrum from one of the Reich's secret factories, his wishes for her speedy recovery, and the promise of another two hundred thousand Reichmarks to go to the coffers of Leni Riefenstahl Film Inc., as well as the use of his own personal Fuehrermaschine. The latter was a medium transport aircraft named *Immelman II*, with which Riefenstahl could scout Alpine locations for the final scenes of the long-overdue and over-budget *Tiefland*. Riefenstahl, trained as a pilot, was already planning to fly herself down to Krün first thing in the morning.

How to say what Riefenstahl felt for this man? The world's greatest power, who removed his boots, knelt beside her, and placed his daffodils on her chest. Riefenstahl is dead, loved, resurrected, healed, worshipped.

She once wrote in her notebook, *Only Hitler heals Leni Riefenstahl's narcissism*. The phrase terrified her. She'd torn out the page.

"I will do it," she said to Isabella, holding the receiver away from her face and staring down the little black holes.

"What?"

"I will fly her to Compiègne."

"But there are projects besides *Penthesilea*, Director. I have some ideas myself."

"Isabella, against all odds, just at the moment Fate says I need a plane, I have a plane. Also, I have a certain knowledge that if only I listen to *something* Novis is saying—"

"Simone Weil."

"—to something *whoever* is saying, I will be my century's Homer."

⇒≫≻ ≺≪⇐

And so that is how, in late August 1941, Leni Riefenstahl flew Simone Weil and Isabella Ahland across the Swiss Alps, 462 kilometres, to northern France in a Junkers Ju 52 trimotor airplane with a turquoise interior.

Below the clouds, it had been one of those bright grey mornings that makes everyone squint more than if the sun were out. But above the white cathedrals, the undiluted sun, in all her inevitable travelling glory, refracted nothing, and the calm clarity of a beautiful void entered the visual fields belonging to Riefenstahl, Ahland, and Weil. Their eyes unstuck and rode the billowing terraces beneath them, and their mouths hung open like the mouths of devouring titans, swallowing the magnitude of the earth.

It was still such a new vantage point, after all. Sometimes the old women in St. John's would quip that the world's young people had been duped into going to war just for a chance to ride in an airplane.

Each of them knew that if the clouds below *Immelman II* parted, no celestial city would rise to meet them. Nor would they find distant and quiet plumes of smoke, the white tents of nomadic barracks, or trenches bitten into the clay. They would see only the impassiveness of green.

"I watched all your films as you requested," Weil said awkwardly in German from the co-pilot's seat, swivelling her head toward the big woman next to her, who was dressed in a white suit with a paramilitary top and skirted bottom, with a leather aviator cap clamped on her narrow head. "Your documentary of the Nuremburg rallies, *Triumph of the Will*, a number of times."

The opening shot of *Triumph of the Will* had been taken from this very plane, flying over white clouds just like these, which parted like a divine curtain to reveal the stone cathedrals of Nuremberg. In this shot, Riefenstahl had invented a new point of view: that of a demigod. Knowing that the audience takes the position not of the actor, but of the camera, and that such identification turns them into critics, she had attached the lens itself to the Führer's frame of reference. Combining omniscience with the limited vision of a man, the perspective descended from on high, then processed through Nuremberg's ancient streets, zooming in, one by one, on the faces of its proud people. The shadow of the airplane on the roofs, the phalanxes decked out in banners and brass, then the convergence: the bashfulness of that woman batting her eyes, the child laughing as she eats an apple, even the cat in the window. The woman, the child, the cat—all the same! *Triumph of the Will* told the story of what the people wanted to look like through their Führer's eyes: unified in their passion.

In the notebook open on her lap, under the title *What to tell Riefenstahl*, Weil wrote: *All her work is about her desire for heaven.*

Riefenstahl dropped *Immelmann II*'s nose below the horizon and coasted him over the mountains at 190 kilometres per hour. The black altimeter ball on the control panel bobbed around its bauble and settled in the middle.

Weil wore overalls, no makeup, her teeth yellow from the constant battery of cigarettes to her lips, her blunt hair unstyled. Those ludicrous round glasses! And clearly, the woman was an anorexic. But Weil's eyes were bright and brown, and in them, Riefenstahl could tell that curiosity outweighed contempt.

Under Weil's gaze, Riefenstahl rose like she did under the judgment of men. She tried to be smarter, eccentric. If only Weil would fall in love with her—the pressure she felt would evaporate, she would win. Now she regretted her red lipstick and crimped hair. In an effort to impress, she said: "You have two and a half hours to tell me everything that will change my life and art. Hold nothing back. Say what you see in my soul."

"I might only need five minutes," Weil said. "What will we do with the rest of the time?"

"As bombastic as me! I like that. Yet I think we are quite different. You're a rich kid, *n'est pas*? You have that ethical faux-poor look about you."

"It's true," Weil said, shrugging a bony shoulder. "My family is rich and has been for generations." She lit her cigarette and inhaled luxuriously, as if she'd just eaten a feast and was now putting up her feet. Still sucking air, she muttered, "I am one of the blessed,"

"Not me—I'm from the bottom of the barrel. I'm completely uneducated. Tell me, how beautiful is Paris?"

"Very beautiful. My parents were sad to leave because of the occupation."

"Ah, but Marseilles is beautiful, too. The Riviera…"

"The refugees…"

Riefenstahl waved one black-gloved hand. "Oh, I don't care what you are. I'm totally ignorant, I don't even know the difference between left and right. I can't be political—I'm an artist! I take no sides, everyone is the same to me. Like Homer, I am impartial."

In her notebook, Weil wrote: *delusions of grandeur really a form of obedience, wants to be what others consider great, will mimic qualities (like impartiality) the moment she discovers they are to be desired, behaves as if she's always had them.* She lit another cigarette, dropped the match onto the open page of her notebook, and watched it smoke.

"What did you just write?" Riefenstahl said.

"That all your work is about your desire for heaven."

Riefenstahl trembled. "It's true," she said, sucking in her long cheeks. "It is so true."

From the corner of her eye, Weil observed this sucking of the cheeks, Riefenstahl's too-close eyes. In her opinion, divinity existed only in the joy of creatures, and in their suffering. She thought that Riefenstahl's desire for heaven distanced her from the suffering of creatures—a grave error that diminished her faith in God and the world right in front of her. But she had a fondness for people who made grave errors.

Meanwhile, in the back of the plane, Isabella sat in one of the seventeen turquoise seats. She stared at Weil over the top of a map of Tanzania, which she'd found stuffed into the pocket under the window, and rhythmically tightened her lips as if chewing a stiff wad of marzipan.

It hadn't been difficult for her to acquire a parachute, helmet, knee and elbow pads from the set of an adventure film. One could throw ten Bofflamots into the crew and nine times hit a velocity addict.

The decision to sabotage Weil's parachute had been much harder.

Isabella had always floated primly and well-attired through life, allowing the world to form itself around her and doing nothing but reflect it back. She judged, but only surfaces. Her role, wherever she found herself, was to be a barometer of what was acceptable and fashionable. It could not be said that her presence was ever enjoyed—even she knew this—but she also knew she was necessary.

But beyond Isabella's proper exterior and perfect, contemptuous taste was shame of the most disobedient kind. Shame that burns the house down. Shame that shits itself in the street.

The only person she really loved was Riefenstahl. Around Riefenstahl, Isabella felt the power and pleasure of self-movement, for Riefenstahl was not a person who floated—she was someone who ran, up bright stone steps to the pantheon on the hill. At the same time, Riefenstahl was broad, gauche, sentimental, a hammer. When she danced, once upon a time, critics had admired her strength and technique, but had found something lacking: the sense normally found in the soul of an artist. It was as though she mimicked passions instead of feeling them. But the desperation with which Riefenstahl aped passion was sincere. Had she been a weaker person, Isabella would have turned from her with scorn. But because Riefenstahl was an Athena of strength and will, Isabella could permit herself to pity and to love her. When Isabella was around Riefenstahl, she allowed herself to feel something true.

Which was why Isabella would ensure that Riefenstahl's loyalty remained unquestioned—a position that would be difficult to maintain if someone found this French activist wandering the wood after having watched her leap from *Immelmann II*. To protect Riefenstahl, Weil must die, and it would have to look like an assassination.

Isabella scowled at Weil's armlet and shifted in her seat. She put a hand on her belt, feeling for her ostomy bag taped to the right side of her navel. Still thin. She sucked in her belly and tried to recede into the distance of her negative space.

That morning, Weil had shown up at the airfield in Dübendorf wearing the blue cotton overalls, cinched leather belt, and red armlet of a member of the Federación Anarquista. Weil and Riefenstahl had stood across from one another on the scorched grass, Riefenstahl's white skirt billowing around her like a spawning dandelion fluff. *Immelmann II* sat beside them with its door open, its corrugated metal skin duller than the slate sky.

"That's a pretty ribbon," Riefenstahl had said, pointing at Weil's armlet. "I wish ours were more that shade of red."

Isabella never really believed Riefenstahl when she played the innocent little savant. She suspected that Riefenstahl's performances of naïveté often endeared her to men of power and allowed her to playfully poke at their most rigid commitments, and the fact that Weil had scowled and slightly recoiled made Isabella nervous. She did not like to see Riefenstahl scolded. Even the suggestion that the White Fairy had been scolded made Isabella's gut start clenching and burning.

"What will people think when they see a Spanish anarchist suddenly walking through the woods?" Isabella had nearly yelled. "Aren't you going to dress like a French peasant or something?"

Weil had just stood there with her cigarette chomped in her teeth, smiling.

"Anyway," Isabella continued, "people don't like to see red when they fly."

Weil pinched her cigarette between her thumb and pointer finger and exhaled slowly. "I suppose red is a mortal colour, and very unlike the sky."

"What a ridiculous observation," Isabella said.

When Isabella had taken out Weil's parachute, she hadn't merely slashed it. Nor had she bunched it up and cut a circle. She was an art director. Over two nights, she had scissored a lacy series of holes shaped like a marigold, so that when Weil pulled the string and the parachute opened but she kept falling, and the faces of all who would suffer at her loss flashed before her eyes, she would look up and see the marigold lit in her parachute like a liquid flame. She would know then that, despite the necessities imposed by the way of the world on the person who did not want to murder her, that person had shown her one last act of gentleness.

Now, in her turquoise seat, with her manicured hands floating on each corner of the map of Tanzania, Isabella wondered whether the flaming marigold had actually been intended to comfort Weil when she looked up or if it was for Isabella herself, when she looked down.

But she felt not an iota of shame or prevarication. The sympathy she had felt for the imaginary Weil shrivelled before the disappointment of the real Weil. Isabella's imaginary Weil had been tall, athletic, and grey-haired, rather like an older version of Riefenstahl. Isabella had always been fond of people older than her. But Weil was exactly her own age, possibly even younger.

Isabella's face reddened, and she cupped her belly. She turned toward the window in order to appear as nonchalant as possible, then sniffed the air, waving her map. Though she was afraid her condition would flare up, as it always did under stress, she had not brought another bag. Still holding the map of Tanzania with one hand, she reached into her purse on the seat next to her and retrieved a vial of Vol de Nuit. Resting it on her thigh, she one-handedly spritzed the black ball of threaded rubber until a vanilla-and-iris web clutched her lap. *If I leak I will kill myself,* she thought.

"It's not quite right, your art director's interpretation of my essay," Weil said, loud enough for Isabella to hear. "Though it is true he doesn't take a Greek or a Trojan side, I did not say the narrator of the *Iliad* is impartial. He is against the shedding of blood, and the fruitless waste of lives for a king's ego. He spares nothing in his representation of brutality."

Cigarette cocked out the side of her mouth, she adjusted her elbow pads, which were too large. Smoke wafted under her round glasses and surrounded her left eye until it was completely invisible, at which point she pursed her lips and sucked it into her mouth.

"You see," Weil continued, muttering the way she did whilst inhaling, "it all comes down to—"

"Oh, I don't think Homer *thought* so much about what he was doing," Riefenstahl interrupted, sweeping her gloved hand across the control panel and then squeezing it into a fist, which she shook in the air. "People who aren't poets often misunderstand how it works. Take my process, for example. I am an infant of the world! Images come constantly at me in a flood, like a gulf on the horizon, opening and spewing a tidal wave toward the sun. They come, but I don't understand what they mean. I am an aperture in the fold of reality!"

Beyond the clouds, a continent of green craters rose and fell as *Immelmann II* passed over the dwindling Alps into the rainy province of Alsace.

"All I've ever wanted to do is create a reality that is more beautiful," Riefenstahl said. After a moment, when Weil did not respond, she snapped, "Isabella, save that perfume for when you're off to an orgy and don't have time to wash your cunt. It gives me a headache."

"Director, why don't you tell her about *Penthesilea*?" Isabella said.

Riefenstahl nodded, relieved. With her arms straight out, pushing her spine into her seat, she began:

"Since 1925, my greatest desire has been to play the part of Penthesilea, the last Amazon queen, from the tragedy by Heinrich von Kleist. Sixteen years ago, at the age of twenty-three, I took a train to my first location shooting for *The Holy Mountain*. That night, as I stood up to leave the dining car, a stocky stranger with a fringe of white hair flipped up like a collar blocked the aisle and, arms spread, cried, 'Penthesilea—at last I've found my Penthesilea!' I do not come from an educated family, so I was totally unaware that Kleist's *Penthesilea* was a major dramatic work that had been playing in Berlin for years. 'Penthesilea, don't you know me? It's the one who loves you, Max Reinhardt.' And so it was. The great director Max Reinhardt, whom I had never met, though I had danced in his theatre."

Riefenstahl clutched her breast and stared off in the distance.

"From that second until the train pulled into Innsbruck, Max told me all about that hard, gripping play. My curiosity was piqued. How could I be someone's Penthesilea if I had never heard the word before? But other events soon took precedence in my life."

She smiled in amazement and also a bit of shyness, her hand stretched before her as though she were a genie bringing a toggle pin to life.

"One year later, I was at a party in Berlin when the Russian stage director Tairov saw me from across the room. He too called, 'Penthesilea! The one, the perfect—half my life I have been looking for you!' Then I knew. These great fathers of the stage had called me by my true name. So, over the next fourteen years, I obsessed over Penthesilea until that naked figure on horseback with streaming hair and a spear in her hand came to seem more real to me, Leni Riefenstahl, and I, Leni Riefenstahl, came to seem like Penthesilea's shadow. Beautiful wild ignorant beast—she came to me in dreams, my twin, not as a human being but as an impalpable creature fashioned by artists! Each of her words, each of her expressions—I had already lived them myself!

"Does anybody know that all of my film successes have secretly been for the sole sake of *Penthesilea*? Once I had enough clout, once I had proven myself—then yes, although the costs are astronomical, the Führer agreed to fund my masterpiece, and I accepted his patronage. I began to train right away. Gymnastics each morning, riding in the afternoons. For me, who had never ridden a horse in her life, it became the most natural thing in the world to jump bareback onto my galloping white mare, Fairy Tale, and to leap over poles four feet high! Every night I worked on the script, but of course I had been working on the script for fourteen years already. The Italian governor of Libya promised me permits for one thousand horsemen and the use of the Libyan desert; I hired the greatest stage director in Germany to direct me in my acting scenes; I very nearly got Leopold III of Belgium to play my Achilles! Then we went to war and all my plans died."

"Many victims of war are children."

"No, please listen, it's something else." Riefenstahl turned her close-set eyes on Weil with the depersonalizing intensity of a baby at the breast. Her red smile stretched across her narrow face. "I don't know what it is. When I heard your essay, I felt a hand reach into me and grip my lungs." Her eyes filled with tears though she continued to smile. Now her voice became high and childlike and her accent rougher. "I have the images—images that have not yet been seen, so unlike Hollywood Technicolour lollipops. Only the subtlest distinctions between beige and brown, like the pyramids against the Nile. A grand battle with white horses under the eternally blue Libyan sky, and the final, tragic encounter between Penthesilea and Achilles against roiling cloud banks. Out on the battlefield she does not recognize him, you see, and she kills her lover, her adversary. Nature will not look realistic—every aspect will be stylized by angles and light and superdimensional views of the sun and the moon, of rainbows and clouds, uprooted trees and plunging waters. But—I don't know what it is. There's a thing, a problem. With the story I think. A problem with the story itself, apart from the film. My dear, are you crying?"

Through a screen of smoke, Weil rubbed her eyes and nose with the same yellowed fingers that held her cigarette. "I'm sorry. It's only that for the first time since I left, I thought about my dear ones. You said *white horses* and my parents and brother walked right into my brain. I told them I was going out to buy a packet of seeds for winter lettuce."

"Hey, what's that speck?" Riefenstahl said.

Through the window of the cockpit, in the blue void over the vale of clouds, a black speck swelled. Riefenstahl tilted her narrow face back and watched the speck advance toward the long bridge of her nose. There was a look of martial arousal in her crossed eyes.

"It's another plane," Weil said.

"Director, you're not flying right at it?"

Riefenstahl laughed, gripping the wheel. "I don't know! That speck is everywhere!"

It was true. In just a few seconds, the speck grew so defined they could make out its propellers. They were the only two machines in such a vast space, yet it seemed they could not avoid each other. But then, while still a ways off, the other plane veered up at a steep incline, and, with a dark flicker followed by a roar, it disappeared over their heads.

Immelmann II bounced up and down in a pocket of mild turbulence. Isabella moaned and Weil went utterly silent and still, but Riefenstahl pounded her thick leg on the floor as if spurring a horse. Then the turbulence ended and the blue void regained its vast serenity and emptiness.

Isabella took off her jacket and wrapped it around her waist. She spritzed herself again with Vol de Nuit, staring straight ahead with an expression of anguish and contempt.

"In Paris I knew a poor family," Weil said in an airless voice, reaching for her tobacco. "Who the parents were, I only saw from a distance. He wore a cap, she had no hair. Four children: a daughter, Ruth, and three younger brothers she took care of. She washed their little hands and faces with the same cloth each time. *The face and hands cloth*, she called it. And while she washed them they all sang, *Face and hands, face and hands*. Totally uninventive. Little chirping birds. She touched all their little noses and said, *Nose, nose, nose*. Touched her forehead to theirs, each in turn at the tub in the yard, and said, *Eyes, eyes, eyes*."

Immelmann II now reached the edge of the great cumulous ocean lapping over the centre of Western Europe. Through thinning mist, Riefenstahl, Ahland, and Weil saw the green-and-ochre patchwork of Champagne's rolling vineyards.

"Their faces were their faces," Weil said to Riefenstahl. "Isn't that beautiful?"

⇶⇶⬤⬤⬤

At exactly that moment, in a wood between the Compiègne Forest and Reims, a mourning dove flexed her breast, batted her tail feathers over the smooth density of her eggs, and, with an ecstatic look in her black eye, swooped down from her nest in the corkscrewed boughs of a dwarf chestnut bent low to the ground. She flitted between the gnarled branches of the grove where she lived and came out of the bramble into a wide avenue of tall, straight, carefully planted trees. Side to side she flapped languorously down the tunnel of white birch and shot up through the yellowing tips to catch a view of the curvature of the earth. Sleeping and awake, this bird was marked at all times by a memory of the horizon. Even though she was a bird, she was drawn to immensity.

⇶⇶⬤⬤⬤

In *Immelmann II*, Riefenstahl said, "Down there, on the earth, do you know sometimes I feel such a springtime horror for everyday things? I might think a flower on my Japanese room partition turns into a tarantula and creeps off the fabric, or that the sun swells in the sky and comes for me. Something happened to me."

"I was wondering," Weil said.

"One winter in the neighbourhood where I grew up—a poor district filled with pigdogs who counted their peas—a child sex-murderer went on a rampage. And one night my father sent me out to the tavern for a pitcher of ale. Oh, he knew about the sex-murderer. But sending me for ale was, I don't know, a way to prick at me and express his discontent. When I returned to the apartment, a man stood shadowed by the dark window on one of the stair landings. As I ran past him up the steps, he grabbed the neck of my dress. I dropped the pitcher, which smashed, and my scream brought the neighbours onto the vestibule. But the man who grabbed my neck—he was gone. And the woman who lived on the ground floor, she hadn't seen anyone go by. So where did he go, if not into the rest of my life, like a stain? He defeated me. And why shouldn't he? He was strong. I was weak. At all costs to myself, I am loyal to nature. But now I am an artist. I ask you, why suffer in art when we suffer in life? I took the hole he made in my little world and transformed it into a vision. All I've ever wanted to do is redeem realism through romanticism."

"Huh," Weil said. "Are you sure there isn't something else? I thought you were going to tell me about your father."

"I did."

"Yes, but—"

Isabella called in a nervous voice from behind the cockpit. "Look, Director. Compiègne."

Beyond *Immelmann II*'s nose, Compiègne stretched its

green tongues to the day. It was a manicured forest that had been planted long ago on a hill, round as an emerald turret with a path running straight up the centre. The forest's breath hung over it in a white cloud.

Weil rose from her seat, her cigarette in her mouth, wobbling under the weight of her parachute. "You're a liar," she said.

"What?" said Riefenstahl.

"You hate nature," said Weil.

She braced her pack against the narrow wall between the cockpit and cargo hold and lowered her brass goggles. Isabella got up from her chair, which was across from the passenger door, and stood by the handle. Riefenstahl reduced power to the engines and gently began to descend.

Out the cockpit window, visible only to Riefenstahl, light broke through the cloud hanging over Compiègne like strings of a nebulous instrument. Anyone who knew Riefenstahl would have taken a second look at the expression on her face. Her jaw was rigid, her eyes locked on a single point far in the distance. Not one person in Riefenstahl's life ever saw her so still.

A familiar scene rolled in Riefenstahl's mind. Against cloud banks on a battlefield of universal woe, the Amazonian queen with flashing eyes pierces Achilles's shoulder with her arrow, separating the tendon from the bone. He falls to his knees and raises his hands. Penthesilea cocks a second arrow as the camera moves over her bronzed and bloody arms, her flat breastplate. Now the music that had been playing diminishes, the sounds of war break behind her. She releases the bow. But wait.

In *Immelmann II*'s cockpit, Riefenstahl frowned. A new shot cut into the scene she knew so well.

Penthesilea sees her mistake. She runs to Achilles but she cannot outrun a shooting arrow. There sits Achilles's head in Penthesilea's hand, staring straight on with one eye. A shaft fills the other socket; the cheek and the beautiful eyelid's crest collapse into the wound. She sits down. She is dazed. She is tired.

Riefenstahl scowled and blinked away tears. She would cry only to get something. Otherwise, no. Out the window, she saw a confounded and perplexed sadness in the desperate green of the hills below.

Just then, a mourning dove crashed into *Immelmann II*'s right propeller. There was a feathery explosion of white and red, and the engine shrieked and clanked. Then the shriek fluted away, the cockpit became one-third quieter, and the plane yawed to the right.

As Riefenstahl bellowed, Weil and Isabella slammed into the passenger door. Holding Isabella's arms, Weil stared into those wide blue eyes. She shrugged out of her parachute.

"Here," Weil said. "Take it."

"No," Isabella said.

"Take it."

"No, I won't."

Weil tottered back and forth with the parachute pressed to her chest. Their two shadows spiraled across the turquoise walls of the cargo hold as the plane completed its circle and continued bearing right.

A third shadow spun around the walls. Riefenstahl stood between Isabella and Weil, her black boots wide apart. She rose a foot above their heads.

"We have lost equilibrium," she said. She flapped her hands at the wrists.

Weil took one last look at Isabella's beautiful, clear eyes. "You must take it," she said.

"No!" Isabella said.

"Here," Weil said again, thrusting the parachute at Riefenstahl this time.

Riefenstahl nodded and took it. In an easy, collected movement, she swung her arms through the straps.

"No, Director," Isabella said.

In two strides Riefenstahl was at the door. She grabbed the lever and pulled it open as Isabella and Weil stumbled out of the way. The plane filled with the flapping roar of wind.

"Leni, stop, you don't understand!" Isabella shouted.

Just then, her fists clutched under each armpit, she remembered a manoeuvre called *raising the dead*, which she had heard the men describe as they told their stories of heroism. Isabella rushed into the cockpit, took the wheel, and banked very slightly left toward the working engines, all while pressing the left rudder pedal. The airflow realigned with the fuselage, and *Immelmann II* regained zero slip angle.

"I'm here, Isabella, you beautiful genius!"

Riefenstahl came up behind her art director, bent, and kissed the top of her coiffed head. "Did you see that quick thinking?" she said, turning to Weil, who stood in the back, holding herself upright with one of the turquoise seats.

Riefenstahl unclipped the parachute from her waist, shrugged out of the straps, and threw it toward Weil. It landed in the aisle like a body.

"I'll fly us to Reims, Isabella. I know exactly where the airport is. Once we circle over Compiègne." To Weil she shouted, "When you see cloud, jump."

Isabella got up and Riefenstahl sat down.

Just before Isabella moved away, Riefenstahl grabbed her elbow and pulled her toward her mouth. Into Isabella's ear, she yelled over the wind, "It isn't that I lack courage, do you understand? Or that I don't love you. It is only that I love myself, objectively. I don't have children, do you understand? I am my own child."

Isabella nodded. Whenever anyone asked her *who are you, what do you do*, she always answered, *I am the White Fairy's conscience.*

She went into the cargo hold, hips swooning into seats, where Weil was struggling to put on the parachute pack, spinning herself in circles every time she pulled the strap at her waist. She patted the wet patch on her blouse where her bag had leaked with sudden fondness.

For the first time that day, Isabella thought of her own child, her Rainart, who for months had been in Dresden with his grandparents. And even when Rainart was with her, nearly every night she had stayed out late: to be with the sparkling lights of her generation, to bask in their radiance before they became truly miserable, once fatigue took from them the supplementary energy that was the source of desire. On those nights, she always said to her husband, *Oh, well. Rainart will be there in the morning.*

Watching her feet drawn slowly along the black rubber lines of the floor, she shyly tried to imagine Rainart's nose. She could not remember its shape with any certainty, or the colour of his eyes. Terror rose in her—the terror of looking up at the empty spot where your child had just been standing.

Isabella fell to her knees before Weil. "I beg you don't go."

Weil looked down at Isabella, with eyes that were very dark and clear. Behind her, out the door, the fields ended at a surf of cloud. They had flown over the forest.

Taking Weil's hand, Isabella got up. She brought her lips to Weil's cheek, and Weil gently pulled one of Isabella's blond curls. Then, turning her face ever so slightly to the left, her mouth soft and open, Weil kissed the German on the lips.

In Isabella's stricken face, in her two large weeping eyes that held the blue destiny of the world, in her naked gums and her chin shaking *no, no*, Weil saw the selflessness that confuses shame.

Weil's crimson cheeks quivered when she pulled away. Gripping Isabella's shoulder, she turned toward the door. She smiled grimly.

"Give me real hell instead of imaginary paradise," she prayed into the wind.

Isabella crouched by the door and hid. She watched her life's most rebellious act pour its aurora of fire on the canvas of treetops below—at least, that was what she imagined it looked like, up close. From the vantage point Isabella shared with the sun, the parachute fluttered dimly, merging with the greyness of the day.

Isabella cowered at the door. She put a hand over her mouth, to keep what remained of her breath from passing over Dresden in two hours' time, spiralling, homesick, in the monarchy of the weather that goes around and around, and infecting her son, in the yard of his grandparents' house, with her quiet metamorphosis into a monster of history.

"I have acted, this is my life's great act," she muttered into her damp and reeking hand.

HANSEL, GRETEL, AND KATIE

IT'S A SORE, RED, INFECTED-LOOKING MOUTH that Katie Wiebe's got, one that contains the terror of her family's end, like she'd gobbled it up only for she couldn't help it, the little witch.

Small as it is, it's a mouth I have to feed.

I became guardian of the Wiebes' toddler right before the war. By the time she came to me, my husband, Derek Pifer, was dead for three years. He'd fallen down a well off in the back sixty and I hadn't gone to look for him on account of he sometimes went for days to auction without telling me. He liked to torture me this way, liked to imagine me trapped by worry and impotence. Me, who didn't get an allowance more than exactly what I needed to keep the house running, and who couldn't go to the bank and make a withdrawal without Derek's co-signature. Not in our town anyway. We followed Company rules, here in the heart of the prairies. Fight and fret him all you want, push him down the stairs, skip his meals, swell up before him in a squall of indignation while he sits at the kitchen table hanging his head and afraid—there is no proving you're his match, Wife, when the facts of the world are against you.

Oh, sure. I was the one who took the cover off that well. Years before he fell down it, though, so by the time he did fall I'd forgotten. Anyway, you can take away a well cover but you can't make a man walk to exactly the place, on the whole two hundred acres, where there's a pit. That was grace delivered me. Then the farm was mine, and suddenly I could go to the bank myself.

I know it's said, *To control a man, give him a plot of land to defend*. This might have been true of me, too, were it not such a hopeless time already. I never quite believed the house might not be taken from me at any moment, didn't feel at home in it on account of it was Derek's inheritance, really. It was somehow thin for a house, just like he'd been thin. In any case, owning this home has not made me compliant.

By then the Company was coming more regular to check on our yields of corn and wheat. They weren't yet interested in the acre of vegetables we all grew to eat and sell at market on the weekends. Really, it amounted to trade, all that selling and buying: zucchini for tomatoes, beans for mushrooms, broccoli for cauliflower. We all grew potatoes, onions, and cabbage, but we brought them to market anyway, for the people from Eireonpolis. They'd sit on these old sawhorses around the barrel of fire Rolf Wiebe used to roast corn, playing at country on their harmonicas.

What is it like to be them, I've always yearned to know. To walk down a sidewalk dressed in the armour of fashion, into a place where I had cause to go and others were expecting me, and where I knew exactly what I needed to do and was good at it?

When the Company eventually took an interest in counting our vegetable yields, we got new contracts we all had to sign—or we didn't have to, but it became illegal to sell to anyone but them, in any case. The weekend markets stopped. What became of the city people then, I'll never know. I suppose some of them became the migrants who started coming through.

After them came the children.

Whoever released them into the wilds did so at first with something like benevolence, for it was still summer then. The children came travelling in their pup packs, ransacking our orchards and berry patches, stealing the odd chicken and bringing it back to the eldest of them who'd set up a sort of camp among the poplars, over in Mustard Woods.

Though people grumbled about their missing stock, we'd all tacitly agreed not to shoot the little scamps, hoping things might rectify themselves when winter came. We told ourselves at the end of the season that, come harvest, there'd be some for us to keep, just like there'd always been. True, we hadn't seen that amount drawn up in our contracts, but the Company wanted farmers, didn't it? It wasn't good business, we said with a degree of self-importance, to have all your workers up and die. I suppose, living on the prairies, we didn't know how full the world was elsewhere, didn't share the general population's dim, panicky impulse to purge itself. No, we were people who conserved, who stocked up.

We had no idea how replaceable we were.

Harvest came, and the Company yielded us nothing.

The Wiebes, though, they resisted. They made themselves a secret pantry in the basement filled with sauerkraut and tomato sauce, potatoes, bags of wild rice, ground corn, smoked turkeys. They plastered it all in behind a fake wall.

But the Company was expecting exactly that kind of sneakiness. They took the entire family outside, Rolf and Sheila and their littlest one, Katie, the one who hadn't run off with the other kids to Mustard Woods. They dug three holes, and into these they put a tied-up Rolf, Sheila, and the toddler, right up to their necks so they were just three heads sticking out of the ground. Rolf and Sheila looked up at us glassy-eyed and mystified, as though the whole thing were a dream, which is how we felt, too.

But when the wee one started to cry, Sheila was beset by an awful clarity.

"Hurry," she screamed at us. "Hurry, for God's sake."

A Company man went over to Sheila, bent down, and untied her thin brown ponytail. Almost lovingly he spread the hair evenly around her face, and then he took a long, straight razor from a black bag he'd brought with him and began to shave her head.

Well, this was too much for us. We sprang forward as a community, knocked the Company man down, dug up Katie, and managed to spirit her away before the Tasers came out and we were all stunned down.

After, there was no sign of Rolf or Sheila. It was as if someone had taken a scythe to the ground and harvested them off. Some of us preferred to believe they'd been sucked into the ground by the field elves, the little people who either helped along the roots or chewed on them with their acidic little mouths, depending on how hungry they were—which of course depended on whether we'd left a tiny patch unharvested. A small waste, symbol of our generosity.

⇒⟩⟩⟩⋟⋞⟨⟨⟨⇐

The toddler, Katie, she came to stay with me because my house was isolated and—even I knew—had the atmosphere of an unvisited place. Oh, it's just an old white farmhouse, like most of them around here. It's got no touches, no tree in the yard, no railing on the front steps. It's perfectly in order, but lean—a dutiful, mean house, unloved, with creaking metal doors that'll pinch your finger if you don't go in and out fast enough. Funny, I suppose, that such a large woman lives in it.

"Oh, you think you'd like the city," Derek once told me. "With everything rushing over your head so you feel small. But you're not a woman who's used to feeling small. Look at this here." He grabbed onto the skin of my thigh.

"Is this your romancing me?" I'd said.

He grinned, somewhat hopeful, somewhat looking afraid of being hit, but it didn't go any further than this. Nor did it ever, since the very beginning. I've discovered I don't like men in this way, or sometimes in any way. But at our best we did share a sibling affection. Well, too bad, I don't think of those kinds of days now.

Katie and I, we were starving. I'd dip a corner of a blanket in the tiny bit of cream we had and let her suck on it for an hour, curled up in front of the pot-bellied stove, as she stared through the little glass window at the scones I had baking in there. Just plain corn and wheat flours, no sugar, to be drenched in milk.

Fat old Esmerelda was my cow and the source of our dairy. We milked her each morning. Katie, little witch, would lean over my knee and try to suckle right onto a teat. Nearly knocked the bucket over every single day. Afterward, she'd slouch around in the dirt while I mucked Esmerelda's stall, piling up manure that come spring I use for fertilizer. Nothing more efficient than a cow, and such perfect sedateness. Peaceful creatures who give everything—their milk, their calves, their manure—and no one ever says, *I just love my pet cow, I'm going to take my pet cow for a ride*. They leave the world unmourned, don't rip anyone's hearts out when they go. That's morality. I must have been the only woman on the prairie who didn't eat beef.

Katie would often cry out for her Mama, or she would say, "Mom? Mom?" when she was curious about an object she hadn't seen before. One time we sat by the stove looking out the window, her on my knee, and watched a large, brilliant meteor exploding in the sky like a fireball. "Mom?" Katie said. Well, if that didn't make me quake in my boots.

"Auntie Gretel," I said. "Say it, Aun-tie."

Katie put her little hand on my breast, more like a claw than a hand, for I hadn't any tool delicate enough to clip her nails. Then her head followed, and she fell asleep snortling into the cracks between her fingers, both hugging me and keeping me at bay.

Of course, I managed a bit of my own sneakiness, we all did, but I was less ostentatious than the Wiebes. I'd built into all my tables—the kitchen table, the end tables in both the bedroom and the sitting room—a false bottom, with planks from some wooden crates I'd had in the yard, and then I'd painted them all, top to leg, entirely in red, which was the only colour I had on account of the barn. Up under those tables went my small stash of dried potatoes and cornmeal and flour and oats.

One day, a narrow Company Man stood with two colleagues at my door.

"Our names are Garnet, Courtenay, and Nibs," he said.

He held up a drill and pressed his index finger into the trigger.

"Your furniture is *red*?" he said when he saw my tables, as if I'd gone and carved my tables from the flayed shanks of bulls.

"Well, to tell you the truth," I said, "my husband, before he died, he was colour-blind, only he would never admit it. He didn't even know what red was—he thought he was painting all the tables chocolate brown. Well, what do you folks think of our grain?"

Courtenay looked side-eyed at hairy-eared Nibs.

"We think it is lucrative," Garnet said. "I am going to examine your walls now."

"I'm on a paleo diet, it's how I stay trim past my prime," Courtenay said. Indeed he was trim, and waxy, with perfect teeth that I believe were replacements, and a non-cancerous, chemical tan.

Nibs was the only one of the three with a bit of chub. He wore a messy burgundy vest. I was wary of gentle Nibs. He sat down in one of my red chairs, folded his hands, and looked at me like I was a sow about to get loaded up on the truck—by which I mean that, though he did not regard me as fully human, he wanted me to like him. A man that well-meaning wants everyone to like him. He'd hand over a broiled little witch on a platter in exchange for a bit of friendship, all the while sadly shaking his head.

Oh, I knew our lives were pathetic to them, and mine more than most, for they could tell I was a person who received little company. What's more, I was the only one in town who was fat. Enormous. Was I gobbling up handfuls of raw grains before they could count my yield?

"Like you," Nibs said, "I'm no stick. Not like my friends here. But it is my duty to tell you that if your predicted yield differs even a little from your actual yield, you will be in breach of contract."

"Actually," I said, "I was born with a special condition where I have the multiple stomachs of a cow. That means I can eat grass, gentlemen."

"Impossible," Courtenay said.

"Well, let me show you," I said, and reefed on the bottom of my dress.

They sprang up and stopped me like I was about to unleash a plague. Sometimes me being a slightly abhorred widow works to my benefit. Multiple stomachs! The idiots.

They gathered up their flashlights, and Garnet his long drill, and they said, "We'll see you in the spring."

Soon as they left, I went and got Katie from where I'd tied her up and gagged her in the hayloft. The poor little witch was crying her head off, of course she didn't understand.

"You're a se–cret," I said, tapping her nose. "Don't you trust the friendly ones, witch."

⇒⇒⤜⤜

That witch, tiny critter, she ate more than me and didn't grow an inch. Where did it go? In that itty red mouth, that's all I ever saw. Every morning I gave her the lion's share of oats or reconstituted mash or cornbread or scones, while enormous me starved. And that was our meal for the day.

I asked her, "Where you putting all that?"

She glared at me with her pale face, lean as bloodless ticks, teeth springing every which way. "Down in the hole," she said.

By mid-December I had gone through everything stashed under the end tables, and was already two-thirds into the last bit left under the table in the kitchen. And then what would I do? I am no hunter.

"Come in the sleigh now, you witch," I said, and the two of us went into the back fields where there's a copse of trees that blocked us from potential eyes travelling down the road. Mustard Woods was in eyesight back there. We sat staring at it and eating a pile of snow, especially the snow crusted with bits of pine cone or acorn shells or smears of frozen sap.

Little witch pointed over the trees in the distance, at the frail tendril of smoke worming up and disappearing into the cold.

"That's the children! Looks like they got a habitation in there," I said.

It made me nervous to speculate any more about what the children were living in or the source of that smoke, in case I guessed a nice, warm cottage and it was actually just a bare fire and some tunnels in the snow.

I grabbed the witch's burgundy, too-big mitt and held her hand on my lap. "Forget about it," I said.

There was a quiet over the prairie then, even quieter than winters had been in the past. The sky's so bright and blue on these prairie winter days it looks fake, like a confection, or paint. It's not as bad to starve when there's a sky like that to sit back and look at. Little witch would have a permissive, if not exactly enchanted, look on her face.

But as soon as the sun sinks a bit, the sky looks real again, thinner and more disappointing, mangy, dim, and then the hunger gets so bad a person could do any savage thing they shouldn't. She'd hunker back far as she could then, into all the old coats and blankets I'd wrap her in. Her eyes had black smudges under them that looked smeared on, and their expression was mean and furtive, like she'd go ahead and clamp those crazed teeth on my ankle as soon as my back was turned.

Well, that malevolent look of hers, and hunger, nearly drove me to commit a crime. I was pulling the little czarina through the fields back to the house on her sleigh. Each time I turned around, wasn't her sullen, mean-eyed face glaring back at me with the pure and unembarrassed hatred of which only children are capable? Witch didn't blink, or if she did, only when my back was turned. It was like she saw me for all I'd ever done, and all I might ever think of doing, in moments of spite.

Now, she is just a child, I told myself. But then, nope. Like thinking, *don't eat the cake, don't eat the cake*, then you black out and suddenly you've gone and eaten eight pieces just before bed.

I gave into bad temptation, the same one that made me go out a few years back and slide off that well cover.

"You little piece of nasty," I said. "Stop looking at me like that or I'll tear off your leg and beat you with it."

Then, next time I turned around, "Who do you think you are? Stinkface, I'll broil a slab of your rump in the oven and you can watch me eat it with a glass of milk."

Every time I looked back at her, the more sour her face was and the more livid I got. So what I did was I dropped the sleigh rope and just kept walking forward. I was so hungry. I thought, she can make it back if she wants to, I'm not pulling her. She makes it back, I'll give her the scone I would've had tomorrow.

What gamblers we are! Never say I don't understand a gambler.

In the back of my mind, I imagined what might be permissible if she just sat there in her sleigh, or wandered around a few feet and then collapsed. Come spring, wouldn't the faces of my neighbours be understanding when I said, well, the toddler, she froze to death. I wouldn't need to say anymore. We'd all have our dark secrets, for we'd have shared the same hard winter, and these trials, they make you forgiving. I wept to think of the silent kindness of my neighbours and of humanity's capacity for mercy.

Then I thought of how different a person seems once they've died, and you perceive them in the context of their life's arc. Derek, for example. We did struggle for power in our relationship, but now he seems so small and pathetic. A little face staring up from the bottom of a well. No, I can't think of it. All those people my age who are gone, those members of my generation who didn't make it. Who'd have thought Sheila and Rolf would go like that, in the blink of an eye, like it was nothing? You think back to being young together and you say nothing ever would have given that person's fate away. Waiting to be struck by lightning, that's life. Do you step here, or do you step here?

Two or so hours later that night, a few minutes after settling into bed, I jolted awake like a sleeper who'd caught herself not breathing. I was covered all in a sweat. Good God, Gretel, I said to myself. What have you done?

I ran back outside to little witch, who sat right where I'd left her, hunched over in the dark with her mittens flat on the ground, and I picked her up and covered her with a million kisses.

"I love you so," I told her. "Auntie would never, never hurt you. You want a scone? I'm going to bake you a scone."

She just hung there in my arms indifferent as a sack but still breathing. She wasn't exactly sweet, that witch, but she didn't hold a grudge either. Oh, was I relieved.

❧❧❧❀❀❀

Since Derek died, it had been my habit to banish him from my thoughts, except for when I'd visit him in the cemetery on his birthday. This was December twenty-third. I would stand before his grave, submit myself to the thin, cutting wind that only wants to freeze your hairs together and trap you in an intricate net of ice and your own composition, and think back upon our life, conscientiously, as a kind of clear and lifting meditation on sadness and guilt. I suppose that was how I confronted taking away the well cover.

But there was no helping it, I couldn't go anymore. I couldn't just tie the little witch to the piano leg and leave her there, nor would I risk bringing her to the cemetery with me, in case anyone drove by. So when Derek's birthday came, I decided that once the witch had gone to bed, I'd sit up into the night and at least do the thinking part of my ritual.

When she went down into her cot, I sat by a little lamp with my hands folded on my lap. At first I was afraid I wouldn't lift because I hadn't gone to the cemetery, but then my thoughts went up like a rocket. I was so hungry, I think I must have disassociated from my physical being.

What I thought about was some years ago, the time Derek grew his hair. I found him before the bedroom vanity touching his bangs, saying, "Well, the guy said I should grow it a little longer, but I'm going to cut it. I'm not having it get out of hand like it is up here."

"That hair makes you look like Prince Charming," I said. "Stop fighting with your own good looks. Every day you wrestle with your beautiful head in the mirror on account of it's too beautiful."

He giggled and ran off into the bathroom. Then he came back into the bedroom entirely naked, with his bits tucked between his thighs so he looked like a Renaissance nude, only with a moustache, and he posed for me with his hands clutched winsomely before his chest and his lips puckered. That was the kind of relationship we had. Friends when we weren't enemies.

Now a man like that, wouldn't he be so sad all alone in a dark hole?

Another thing I think about is how he resigned himself. I imagine it was by falling asleep. Just sleep, little one. This is what I thought of: him sleeping all alone in the wet and dark, and I wept.

Then the clock struck midnight, and I said, "Happy Birthday, Derek, I'll see you again next year."

I got into my nightdress and was about to hop into the cot next to little witch, when I looked up and saw a pale face staring at me through the kitchen window. Well, I didn't even scream, I thought I was having a hunger vision.

"Go away, Derek," I told it.

Time for bed, I thought. Then I thought, Oh hell, better check if this really is a ghost. Walked across the kitchen, yanked open the back door. Indeed, there was a critter. I grabbed it by its scruff and threw it into the house.

"Who are you?" I said.

"Hansel Wiebe," the child said, and burst into tears.

Well, this woke up his sister. She sat up in the cot and rubbed her eyes. She took a good long look at him, her own kin, and said, "Hot dog?" The cannibal.

Of course, I considered it. Him with his little face scrunched up and crying, crying, crying not for danger but for he knew he had no one to love him. If only to put him out of his misery, I thought, why not bake one solitary hot-cross bun that I say is just for him? And then when he's gaping at it, push him in the oven. At least his last feeling would be one of mouth-watering hopefulness.

But then I thought, no, that would be his second-last feeling.

I told Hansel Wiebe to sit down at the kitchen table and warm himself. I bent down and pulled off his boots, his layers of mittens, his four hats. Who knows when the critter had last been undressed or washed, it was so cold out. And him still so young and sweet, his feet and hands didn't smell like skunk at all.

"And where are the other kids?" I asked.

Hansel Wiebe beamed his weepy eyes right at me. "Hunted," he whispered.

Behind me Katie started to cry, as if she knew what the word meant.

"Now shush," I said, hanging Hansel's things up by the stove. "It's perfectly okay, you little dramatist."

I didn't ask who was doing the hunting, didn't know, didn't want to. Young men, I imagined. None of them parents, too lazy or ignorant to go the long distance to hunt for deer. Just like I'm no parent. And I, too, wasn't about to go bivouacking for three days east into the Shield on the trail of a buck, not in my state of hunger and fatigue. I am, after all, a solitary, unloved widow of supernatural enormity who's not particularly renowned for kindness. The same children being hunted in Mustard Woods, they used to run by me at market and yell, "Witch!" until their parents smacked them. Maybe everyone will say it was me.

Oh, I was so hungry. The kind of hunger that flares into your chest then disappears, leaving you exhausted, with almost no feeling at all, as if you're in water the same temperature as your own body—but then in the midst of all that nothing, when you least expect it, the hunger yaws open again, rips you apart in the middle. A perfectly nice person transforms into a werewolf.

I cooked up a small pot of oats. "Eat this here," I told Hansel. Sat across from him and watched him shovelling until I thought drool would start spouting from my face like a fountain. Got up and stood by the stove, sucking the inside of my cheeks. Rolled my tongue around like it was an overcooked piece of mutton in need of softening.

After, I put a pile of blankets down in front of the stove and said to Hansel, "Now, that's for you."

I was so famished I thought I was floating. Floated into the cot next to little witch, floated the cover over my head—I swear my chest was barely lifting. Air just seeped into me.

"You're snoring," Hansel said from the floor.

"Bet there's no snoring to disturb you outside in the woods," I said.

"I was just remarking," Hansel said. "It's nice to hear indoor noises again." Then he started to cry, deep and bitterly, all to himself—gulp, gulp, gulp.

I nodded right off, too fatigued to console a cactus much less a child. Yet I couldn't sleep. I just floated in the dim sea of the night, surfacing like a whale to peer out at the fire consuming itself through the oven window, casting orange shadows across my hanging pots and bare walls, as though a sunset had detached itself from the sky and decided to remain at exactly the point on the horizon where it doesn't hurt your eyes to look at it. A prairie is an ancient, dried-up seabed, and I swear in my hunger I was floating in the ghost of the waters that used to be here, sipped upon by dinosaurs. Drifting off into extinction as dreamily as that would be delightful—but I don't believe that is how one starves to death.

Then it was dawn. The room was frigid, a flat white light coming through the kitchen window. I bounded up out of the cot like I'd been stung, ran outside, and grabbed a pile of wood for the fire, tore off pieces of bark and chewed on them. It was just frozen poplar but it tasted marvellous, exactly like cinnamon.

The children raised themselves onto their bony elbows and stared at my chewing on a log. Their faces looked half-caved-in with weariness, black-and-red craters below their eyes. Little witch blinked ever so slow, confounded to find herself still alive in this world and in my kitchen, but lacking the necessary enthusiasm to feel either happy or afraid.

"All our eyes are so wet, we look like frogs," Hansel said.

My stomach rumbled at the mention of frogs. "Shut up." My tongue was so thick and slow, I almost tried to spit it out.

I put together the flour, lard, and water for two scones and set them baking. "One for each of you. Take them out when they're done," I told Hansel, who watched me with a grim, guilty expression.

"What about you?" he asked. Blessed kid.

"Is that shutting up?" I said, eating raw dough out from under my nails. I put the mixing bowl in the sink, stumbled over to the peg, grabbed my coat, and set off for the barn with the milk bucket.

Esmerelda was stomping around, chewing on her hay bale, happy and fat as ever. I collapsed onto the milking stool and started pulling her teats. Milk and steam hissed out, and before I knew it I was licking it right off my hands. Then I was picking up the bucket and chugging all I'd gotten so far. Threw up right in the milk bucket, which gave me a sudden relief, and drank it again. With a sigh, I rested my head on her flank and milked her till she was empty. Put the bucket just outside her stall where she couldn't kick it over, snatched down a pile of blankets I had up in a closet from when Derek and I had horses, wrapped myself up like a sausage roll, and fell asleep next to Esmerelda's stall in the big pile of hay.

Hours later, I woke so stiff and cold I felt mechanical. My mouth possessed the infantile taste of milk and bile, and my bowels were pained, suddenly, into quivering. I stomped outside and squatted around back of the barn, propping myself up with an empty gasoline barrel. Went back for the milk bucket and shivered my way back to the house.

The back door to the kitchen was flung open. Hansel and Katie stood in the doorway, waving at me like I was a princess in a parade.

"What?" I said.

"Come in, come in," Hansel said, bowing in the manner of a little French page.

"Course I'm coming in," I said.

Set out on my red, rectangular slab of a table were about half a dozen pots filled with the congealed remains of the rest of my boilable stash: my oats and reconstituted mash and cornmeal. There was an empty white bowl at the head of the table, and four spoons radiating out from either side of it, arranged by size from large to small. Wooden spoons stuck out rigid as porcupine quills from the contents of each pot. Hansel took my free hand and pulled me toward the table. I set the milk bucket on one of the unoccupied chairs.

"May I take your coat, madam?" Hansel said. He yanked on it and it fell right off me and onto Katie, pinned her to the floor. Witch made a close-mouthed moaning noise I believe was giggling. Hansel picked it up and carried it over to the peg. He stood on his toes to hang it, but when he realized his attempts were futile, he folded it ever so carefully in half and set it down on the floor over some of Derek's old boots, as if it were a baby being laid in a crib.

"Sit," little witch said in her low, rasping voice.

I sat. Hansel came and scooped out a pile of oats into my bowl, pile of mash, pile of polenta.

"Now you do this," he said proudly. He took up the big spoon next to my bowl and stirred it all around for me. Then he carefully put the used spoon down in front of him and moved my row of clean spoons up one spot closer to the bowl, bent over them like he was cracking the atom.

"You eat?" I said.

"Not yet. We were waiting," Hansel said.

I just grunted. Lustfully, with a great deal of restrained violence, I dipped in my utensil and shovelled a hunk of mush into my mouth. Soon as the food hit my tongue, my stomach lurched alive with a roar. I shovelled and shovelled. When I got empty, I snatched up the pot of oats and ate what was left right off the wooden spoon. When that was gone, I grabbed the pot of reconstituted mash, then the pot of polenta. I was a juggler of pots. Let rip one thunderclap of a burp.

"Wash up," I growled. "And put a couple logs on the fire."

Darkness pressed against all the windows, persistent as oblivion. I got up, walked the stairs to my room and sat for a moment at the end of my bed. Didn't say excuse me, didn't say I'd be back soon. Just had to get away right then.

I sat on the edge of my bed feeling very afraid of myself and of what I might do.

It was cold up there, and dim—only a bedside lamp shone from one of those ransacked side tables. There was a feeling of large, expectant emptiness, as I hadn't slept at all in this room since bringing home the witch. Barely came up here now, and if so, only to stick my head in and absorb some of the nostalgia that waited deadly inviting. In the black rectangle of the window, there was just me—slouched, with a grey bun that looked torn from a rabbit's derrière and pinned to my head—and the yellow orb of the lamp, and above it, a paler, smaller orb, which was the moon. I heard Derek's little voice somewhere off in the left corner of my brain.

I know it was you, he said. *I know it, I know it.* How repetitive, the dead!

Forgive me, I said in my mind.

No, Derek said.

Please, I said.

Maybe, he said.

I laid myself back on the paisley quilt, straight and perfectly neat with emptiness, and shut my eyes.

꙳꙳꙳

I jolted awake, freezing. Shot right up. Oh my, I had a feeling I'd been asleep for years, and everything I dreaded to lose had been lost. But it was all pretty much the same as before I'd sawed off: the moon, the same stillness, stove glow reaching between the banisters. Same force looming at the bottom of the stairs. The gravity people give off when you're fond of them.

I crept to the top of the stairs and peered around the newel post. Down there, that Hansel was ladling some milk out of the bucket into a mug. A few small lumps plopped out from where my bile had turned it, and he sniffed it, shrugged, and tipped the mug against the red mouth of his sister. Milk dribbled all down her chin as she clacked her jaws around, staring up at her brother with those eyes of indiscernible colour, staring with great regard, if not fondness. I watched them for a moment, then went back to my room.

Up from the back of my closet, I took down a blue-and-gold tin. It was a box sent to my mother when I was a child, from her father in Nuremberg. This grandfather of mine, I never did meet him. He was a bad man. But he liked fine things, and he painted, too. He sent us three paintings: an austere one of a winter landscape by a river; one of two girls in blue dresses in the woods, hunting for berries; and an awful one of an old peasant woman's face hooded in a dark shawl, set against a blackened rust swirl, as though she inhabited a furnace. The paintings were frightful and sad and sufficient as art, but there was something wrong with each of them. The young girl's forearm reaching for berries was too long. That old, hooded woman, my mother said, was actually a man. And the landscape had a blob on it that seemed like a fuzzy, half-formed goat, but you let your eyes drift and you saw it was supposed to be a patch of whitened meadow through the trees. Guess he hadn't figured how to keep the background in its place—it sprang out at you when it shouldn't. Other than painting, he'd been a farm labourer, just like the rest of us.

The box, I don't know why I kept it. Dark magic, I think, for my grandfather was bad, but he did paint. Anyhow, he sent her this box, and in it was one of those Old World, make-it-yourself gingerbread houses—the hard, spicy kind that never moulds.

I pried open the box, got a whiff of nutmeg. The brown slabs were stacked up, arranged by shape. Just like they'd always been, for first thing my mother did when she got this box in the mail was open it, shut it, and put it up in her own closet. There were little silver balls, ones that tasted of anise, and some hard, white, lacy icing for shingles. It was a rather simple candy house, dulled with time as if it had been left out in the sun, which is, of course, exactly the opposite of what had occurred. Rather, I think lack of observation had leached its vibrancy, and it'd begun to merge with the dark loneliness of the inside of the box.

I carried the tin down the stairs like it was a pigeon on a platter. The kids stared up at me with their big eyes both obedient and rebellious. "Couldn't trust you to throw you," I told them. Put on my coat and boots, took up the tin again, and walked out the kitchen door.

It was cold blue and windless outside, an enormous moon, the kind that'll keep you company, just like your footsteps crunching in the snow or your breath spooling out of your head in a thin fog keep you company. This deadly beautiful season, all your tiny interactions with the world swell up in their discomfort like spirit companions and detach themselves from the rest of you. The aura of your breath and coldness of your fingers so hard to believe, the sounds of your footsteps come just a smidge too late, like someone else is making them. You wonder at the dia-mond glistening of night, a feeling so vast and innocent it's like being possessed. It's the season makes your own death seem a strange and lovely place you might wander into, like a woman I once heard of who got out of bed, walked into the middle of a frozen lake under the moon, and fell through a hole in the ice, straight down and silent. How'd anyone know it happened? In spring her nightgown rolled in some driftwood. But for the rest of her, she may as well have been whisked off by aliens into another dimension.

Ahead was the barn, almost indigo in the light. I slid open the door and went into the dark moistness of it. Flicked on the bulb. There was Esmerelda chewing on her hay bale, softly grunting, head steaming, flicking her tail out of happiness for the surprise to see me at that hour.

"Oh, my girl," I cooed.

I brought the tin over to her. Fed her slabs of hard cookie out of my hand, walls of the house never made. My ancestral home, I suppose. Made me sad to think that.

Esmerelda's ears swivelled forward, her eyes scorched with fear of this rare treat she gobbled with desperation, even hysteria, all the gingerbread walls and white candy shingles and decorative silver balls. Surely it was the most delicious thing she'd ever tasted, her just a plain old jersey cow in a lonely barn on a silent prairie, property of a woman herself unloved. No creature was ever more utterly pristine of attachment. Stroke the cheek of Esmerelda, you'll have a feeling of purity and freedom, like drying a handmade plate, so pretty and unremarkable and necessary.

It was exactly the opposite feeling I had holding that little witch on my lap. Her so crazily solid and heavy with the love I felt, I could never believe it. I would squeeze her till she had to squirm away. Oh, these lovable creatures. They are wicked things, sure.

I cut Esmerelda's throat, deep and quick so she never knew.

꙳ꚰꚰ꙳

Yes, this is how we three survived the winter. Eventually I hung her in pieces. But on that night, I collected her blood in the milk bucket, and I boiled it with a little wheat flour and salt to make a loose sausage. The children, they were silent and careful around me, and I cannot say I was sweet to them. They made a noise, I said, "Shut up and eat."

I don't know they'll think of me fondly much when they grow up, but I do my best. For better or worse, I kept us human.

ACKNOWLEDGEMENTS

Thank you to my friends and family for love, and for being so interesting: Gerburg, Ian, Susanne, Len, Chaliz, Barb, Wally, Cher, Tiffany, Bryan, Chris, Janet Squirrel, Ken, Jaclyn Monkey, Crista Minx, Cara, Seanna, Derek, Aynsley, Emily, Talia, Erin, Marina, Filipe, Joel, Sean, Rena.

To Uta for her shelves of books.

To Helen for her cigarettes and love of Emerson.

To Emily and Julienne for sharing the intimacies of new motherhood and for your brilliant minds.

To Alyson Brickey for Sunday swims, intellectual jousts, long walks, for being family.

For helping me find the best part of myself: my little Milt, Julie O'Rourke.

To Ann and Dave O'Rourke.

Thank you to my siblings in the art spirit:

To the 2009 summer workshop with David Mitchell at the Humber School for Writers, and to the 2014 University of Toronto Writer in Residence workshop with David Bezmozgis.

To David Mitchell.

To my teachers, classmates, and students at Sarah Selecky Writing School, especially Jennifer Manuel.

To writing groups past and present, especially to Kasia Juno, Brendan Bowles, Laura Hartenberger, Annie Russel, Michael Collins, Keith Cadieux, Barbara Romanik and Joanna Graham.

To my Winnipeg Reading Group!

To Andrew Forbes.

For early encouragement: thank you, Suzanne Zelazo.

For guidance, inspiration, and lessons on letting go: thank you, Sarah Selecky.

For generosity, mentorship, and for cutting through: thank you, David Bezmozgis.

For energy, kindness, attention, recommendations, and learning: thank you, Zsuzsi Gartner.

To the Writers' Trust of Canada, especially Mandy Hopkins.

Thank you to my extraordinary editor, Bryan Ibeas, for your odd tastes, your generosity, your wise instincts, for taking a chance.

To Leigh Nash, for rigour and authority that makes us all feel reassured.

To Jay Young, for the love and the years.

For your mirth, capaciousness, pragmatism, for giving me a home in the world, for your acting: Aimee Parkes.

To Natalie Malla for hilarity, moral guidance, power, for days of writing together, for being my home, for your films.

To Liz Harmer, a first reader, for kindred demonism, a wide heart, inspiration, intensity.

To my little heart, Charlie.

Most of all thank you Jason, rarest spirit, favourite pair of eyes, for everything.

INVISIBLE PUBLISHING produces fine Canadian literature for those who enjoy such things. As a not-for-profit publisher, our work includes building communities that sustain and encourage engaging, literary, and current writing.

Invisible Publishing has been in operation for over a decade. We released our first fiction titles in the spring of 2007, and our catalogue has come to include works of graphic fiction and non-fiction, pop culture biographies, experimental poetry, and prose.

We are committed to publishing diverse voices and experiences. In acknowledging historical and systemic barriers, and the limits of our existing catalogue, we strongly encourage LGBTQ2SIA+, Indigenous, and writers of colour to submit their work.

Invisible Publishing is also home to the Bibliophonic series of music books and the Throwback series of CanLit reissues.

If you'd like to know more, please get in touch:
info@invisiblepublishing.com